T0375708

A Deadly Obsession

Clarence Willis

AuthorHouse™
1663 Liberty Drive
Bloomington, IN 47403
www.authorhouse.com
Phone: 1-800-839-8640

© *2011 Clarence Willis. All rights reserved.*

*No part of this book may be reproduced, stored in
a retrieval system, or transmitted by any means
without the written permission of the author.*

First published by AuthorHouse 4/18/2011

ISBN: 978-1-4567-4508-0 (e)
ISBN: 978-1-4567-4509-7 (sc)

Printed in the United States of America

*Any people depicted in stock imagery provided by Thinkstock are models,
and such images are being used for illustrative purposes only.
Certain stock imagery © Thinkstock.*

This book is printed on acid-free paper.

*Because of the dynamic nature of the Internet, any web addresses or
links contained in this book may have changed since publication and
may no longer be valid. The views expressed in this work are solely those
of the author and do not necessarily reflect the views of the publisher,
and the publisher hereby disclaims any responsibility for them.*

This book dedicated to
Hilda K Willis
whose encoragement made it all possible

Chapter One

The rain had finally stopped and there were no clouds in the sky. It had been raining off and on for the last three days of Josh's vacation. Josh and Mary had rented this same beach home for the past five years. It was a two family home directly off Tampa Bay in Clearwater, Florida.

This was their first year to have the luxury of a boat. Josh bought the boat and motor during the first week of their vacation in Florida. The water around Clearwater was perfect for fishing and boating and Josh loved to do both. Most of his friends that vacationed in Florida had boats and he wanted one to join them in their boating and fishing days on the Bay and on the Gulf of Mexico.

Josh had used all of his savings and borrowed to his limit on two credit cards to purchase the boat and motor. He was certain that he would soon be able pay them off. He had just recently been promoted to a management position and his pay had been increased significantly.

He had not expected his boating startup expenses to be as high as they were. First; he had to buy many accessories such as life preservers, nets, ropes, and bumpers. Secondly; after he purchased the boat and motor he discovered that docking privileges in Florida, especially those with access to Tampa Bay and the Gulf of Mexico were very costly.

To play with the Florida millionaires he found it very costly, but was committed to the expense now. As soon as he could handle the additional cost of a trailer, he had reasoned that would save him money in the future, because he would no longer have to pay the expensive docking and storage fees. This would also allow him to trailer the boat to his rented home avoiding all the docking fees and he could use the boat back home on the Michigan lakes.

He had missed paying his last two credit card payments, but now that these onetime expenses were out of the way, he should be able to get everything back to a current status when he got his next two paychecks.

The family was eating breakfast, and Josh said, "Looks like we can have one more day on the boat before we have to pack up for home. We can go up the Bay to Dunedin and have lunch at the Bon Appetite."

Nancy and Billy objected, they wanted to go to the beach.

Mary reminded him that they were to meet Henry and Sarah, a couple that lived in Clearwater year round, at the Largo Elks lodge for dinner and dancing , so they would have to be back from the beach by four or four thirty at the latest.

Josh told them that he would have them back in time to take them over to the beach for at least three or four hours.

Mary added, "That sounds like a good idea. Maybe we can all soak up a little sun along the way. I would hate for us to go back up North without a little tan."

Little Billy said, "Daddy can I steer the boat?"

"No, Daddy, its' my turn; Billy steered it the last time." His sister Nancy yelled.

"Well I tell you what; Billy, you steered it home the last time we went out so Nancy can steer it up the Bay and you can steer it back again; how about that?" All agreed that was a fair arrangement.

Mary got up to clear the table and returned with the coffee pot after turning on the small TV that was on the kitchen counter. When the TV screen appeared, there was a panel of three men discussing the rising unemployment rates. That same topic had been discussed every day over the past two months.

Josh said, "Damn it, can't they find something else to talk about? They have everybody scared to death. The Democrats blame the Republicans and the Republicans blame the Democrats, and the Independents blame them both. I'm fed up with hearing about it all the time. Why in hell can't they all get together and fix the problems. I think they all need to be voted out of office."

Mary told Josh that he should watch his language when the children were present. Josh agreed and said he was sorry.

Billy asked, "Daddy is damn a bad word?"

Nancy told Billy, "Don't be stupid Billy you know damn is a bad word. Stevie says it all the time and his daddy spanked him for saying it."

The news commentator reported that unemployment was approaching 10% with all indicators pointed to even higher rates. Josh's home state of Michigan was already exceeding 12%.

"Do you think that there is any chance you may be laid off Josh? Helen told me on the telephone yesterday that George had been laid off just last week and he works at the same plant you do?"

"Not a chance Mary Louise, I think the damn TV people keep stirring it up all the time and have people scared to spend money and businesses scared to hire new employees. George was in manufacturing. The company just had to let a few employees on the line go, because sales were down since GM sales fell off. I'm in management and not on the line. If I had not gone into management I would have to worry. Thank goodness I accepted the new position."

"By the way, I have to call Jim at the Marina, to make sure that our boat will be in storage until we come back next winter. I hope we can get a spot where the sun doesn't shine on it all afternoon."

"Do they have any spots in the building that are in the afternoon shade Josh? Isn't that expensive? Do you think that having a boat down here for four weeks every winter is worth the expense?"

"Well yes it is costly now, but as soon as I get the boat partially paid for, I will get a trailer and we can take it back home every winter so we can use it on all the lakes around Michigan during the summer months up home. Won't that be fun? They have lots of room in the covered sheds and I'm sure I can find one in the shade."

"Yes Josh, but perhaps we should have waited to buy the boat until we had the money to buy the trailer. Just how much would a trailer cost?"

"One big enough to carry our size boat would be around $4,500."

"Josh, what would we do if you did lose your job?"

"Damn it to hell Mary Louise, I told you that I am not going to lose my job, so quit worrying about that. Let's get ready to have some fun and go up the bay to Dunedin."

After a morning of boating on Tampa Bay they arrived at the docks of the Bon Appetite restaurant just after twelve noon. They ate their meals and Josh offered his credit card to pay the bill. The waiter returned later and asked if he could talk with Josh. Josh left the table with the waiter and was told that the bank had refused his card.

Josh yelled, "That can't be true. I just sent them a payment." He was then offered the telephone to use if he would like to call the card company. He took the phone and said, "Maybe I am over my limit. I have been spending a lot of money down here in Florida," Then he called the card company. They told him that he was over his limit and because he was still past due with one payment they could not authorize him to exceed his limit. He was told that he had been late on his last two payments. He told them "Yes, but I did send one to you didn't I? I have never missed a payment before."

"Yes we received that but you are still one payment behind and this charge will put you over your limit. Our company policy will not authorize this payment. Sorry."

Josh hung up the phone and returned to his table and asked Mary if she had any cash with her?

"Yes, how much do you need?"

"Twenty dollars will be enough." Between Josh and Mary they came up with enough to pay their luncheon bill. After leaving the restaurant Mary asked Josh what all of that was about?

Josh told her, "I forgot that I was so close to my credit limit on that card and they wouldn't pay the bill." He didn't mention that the real problem was because he had been late in paying the last two payments on the card.

"You're lucky that I had my purse with me. You have a credit line of $25,000 how in the world can you be over that limit?"

"I needed more cash than I thought to finalize the boat deal when we got down here."

"You mean you borrowed money on your credit cards to buy the boat. You told me that you used only money from our savings account to buy it."

"I did, but I needed a little more than we had in saving."

"How much more, what did that boat really cost?" she asked.

"It cost $37,000."

"You mean you paid $37,000 for that boat and motor? Are you crazy? You told me it would cost us only $20,000?

Josh how could you do that when the mortgage on our house takes almost half of your pay check every month? We have a big car payment to make on top of that? Just where did you expect to get the extra money?

Why did you lie to me Josh? If you used all of our savings account to buy the boat I hope you didn't take any money from the children's savings account. Did you Josh? I pray that you didn't do that for this damn boat? That savings account was for our children's college. Remember, that $10,000 of that account was from my mom and dad to start a college fund for them.

Did you use any of that? If you did I want you to sell that boat right now."

"Yes, but only $9,000 of it. I'm sorry, Mary Louise, I thought we could handle it. I'm sure that I can get everything back in order soon. I'm sorry that I lied to you, but I was so enthused with the prospect of having a boat down here every winter when we came down, I'm afraid I let my dream get ahead of good judgment. Yes, I think you are right. I will put the boat up for sale tomorrow. I realize now that was a stupid thing to do."

"Tell me the truth Josh, what else have you not told me? I had a call from the bank before we left home that you had not made your payment on the mortgage. When I asked you about that you told me that you had sent it that day?

"Are we also behind on our mortgage? Will we have to sell the house too? Just get us back to shore so I can't handle any more of this. You can call Henry and cancel out tonight. I am fed up with your constant overspending. You now have us in one hell of a fix."

They were still discussing their financial position when they got home.

Josh was getting upset. "Damn you Mary Louise, I have told you a dozen times that I can handle the situation, I just got promoted and my new salary will get me out of debt real soon."

"No, Josh, you just can't handle it - you just can't stand not being able to keep up with your friends Henry and John. They both own their own businesses and are both probably millionaires. You just can't keep up with them even with your increase in your paycheck trying to be Mr. Big Shot, your nothing but a Mr. Big Shit." Mary was so upset she was trembling and crying.

Josh replied."I might be a big shit in your eyes, but in my eyes, you're a little wimping bitch. You don't think I can I handle anything, last month you called an electrician to fix that switch and paid $75.00 for a job that I could have fixed myself. How's that for spending foolishly?"

"That's true, but when would you get it fixed Josh? I had already waited over a month and the garbage disposal didn't work."

"I was busy working in my new position. I was working late if you will recall. I'm tired of your bitching, you are my wife and you will do exactly as I say you will. I have always paid my bills on time. Quit fussing over the money or I will kick your ass out of this house and the one back in Michigan as well." Josh was standing in front of Mary and raised his hand as if he was going to strike her.

Mary pushed him away from her and he then struck her in the face. Her nose began to bleed. She ran to the bathroom and locked the door. Yelling ,"That's it Josh, you have hit me for the last time."

Josh, knowing that he was wrong, went to calm the children who were both crying and yelling for him to quit hitting their mommy. He tried to comfort them but they ran away from him. He went to the bathroom door and said, "I'm sorry sweetheart, I'll never do that again."

Mary threw a bar of soap at the door and said, "Your damn right you won't. I won't be around for you to hit." She came out of the bath holding a wash cloth to her nose and took the children by the hand then led them all to the bedroom. She locked the door behind her.

Josh was truly sorry that he had hit Mary. He got little sleep that night on the sofa. He agreed to himself that Mary had been right about him. He had to get things corrected and soon.

He wrote a brief note to Mary "I'm sorry sweetheart that I lost my temper. I am indeed a big shit as you called me. I promise I will never hit you again. I'm going to the boat dealer today and I will sell the boat. We will leave for Michigan tomorrow morning. Pack our bags while I am gone and I will load them in the car when I get home so we can leave early in the morning. I love you! "

When he arrived at the Marina Boat Sales he told the dealer that he had to sell the boat right away, and asked if he would he handle the sale for him. The dealer agreed to handle the sale; but told Josh, he would not be able to sell it as a new boat.

"A boat is like a new car, but actually worse. As soon as a boat is sold a third of its value is lost when the boat is first placed in the water. I will try to get you

$25,000, and my sales commission will be ten percent or $2,500. It may not sell for more than $20,000, but I won't sell it for less than $25,000 without calling you first." Reluctantly Josh agreed, and the consignment papers were signed.

On their trip back to Michigan, Josh kept talking about his plans to resolve their personal problems and what else they could do to get their financial position back on track. Mary said very little on the entire trip.

Josh had already told her that they would forego the beach house next year and that he did not leave a deposit for the following year as they had done on the past five years.

Mary finally spoke and told him, "You didn't have the money to pay it anyway."

Josh did not reply to Mary's statement but said he would sell their second car. It would not sell for much more than $1500, but they would be able to cancel the insurance payments on it and that would get his credit card up-to-date. He figured that if they sold the boat, even at the expected loss, they could surely get everything right again.

His real concern now was how they could build up the children's college savings account again. Billy, the older of the two children, jumped into the discussion and said, "Daddy, don't worry about my college money, I don't need to go to college." and little Nancy joined her brother and said, "Me neither daddy."

Josh looked at Mary and saw that she was crying. He too had tears in his eyes.

"Don't worry kids, we will have your money back real soon." They arrived home in Michigan and it was just beginning to snow.

After stopping at a restaurant for a meal, they unpacked their car and showered. Mary was still not talking to Josh. She went to bed without saying a word to Josh. When Josh came to bed, he turned to her and attempted to comfort her.

She simply turned away from him saying, "Not tonight Josh, I am in no mood for further discussion on this matter with you. Ever since you got that promotion to management, you have tried to play the part of a big shot, and you attempt to play like you were a big shot. If our children don't have funds for college, I will never forgive you. I will find it hard to believe you ever again."

Josh said no more that night. He left the next morning without breakfast before Mary got up. He left a note saying that he was going to sell their second car and that he would be home later.

After Mary had breakfast, she went to Josh's desk in the den, and found the file where Josh kept his credit card bills. She was examining the bills to see just what had been charged over the last several months to exceed his credit limit. She found a charge for a motel room. She would surely ask Josh about that. They had never stayed in a motel in Midland and they had no reason to rent a room when they had a four bedroom house.

Then on an earlier bill there were two more charges from the same motel. The total charge for the three entries was over $200.00. She wrote that down to question Josh about them.

She began thinking about those charges and remembered that Josh was not coming home from work some nights after he was promoted. Prior to his promotion he was always home at the same time. He was never late for a meal. Her feelings for Josh began to worsen. She was certain that Josh was having an affair with someone? She was going to file for a divorce. She was sure she had grounds now.

Josh came home late in the afternoon and told Mary that he had not found a buyer for the car yet. He would try again the next day.

Mary was still very upset. She asked Josh about the motel bills that had been charged to their credit card.

"Damn it Mary Louise have you been going through my papers?"

He immediately regained his composure. He needed to address this new matter carefully.

"The girl in our office needed a place to stay when her husband came home drunk one night, and I rented the room for her and used my card. She paid me back on her next payday."

Mary, yelled, "Did he come home drunk two other times?"

Josh was now aware that Mary had caught him in a lie and she was not going to listen to any more lies. She had found about his affair with a whore that he had met at a bar one evening on his way home from work.

He had to think of something fast and finally lied once again "No, Mary, I rented the room for business reasons. We held several meeting's in the room. The company reimbursed me later." Mary knew he was lying.

"Josh, you are lying to me, and you know you are. Who was she Josh? Company business my foot! I know what you were using that room for. I was worrying myself sick trying to figure out how we could get our bills all paid and get things back to normal. Now I find out that you have been messing with some woman. Probably a whore you met at one of your bars."

"Now you have given me something else to worry about. Have you given me Aids or some other disease? Was she a stinking whore Josh? Were you so hard up that you had to screw a whore?"

She did not give him time to answer. "I have had it with you. I want you out of this house tonight. I will file for a divorce tomorrow. How could you have done this to me?"

She would not talk with Josh or answer any thing he asked of her and she went to the bedroom and slammed the door to her room.

Josh gathered up some of his toiletries and clothing and left. He slammed the door loud so Mary would know he was gone. He was certain that he and Mary could still work out something after he had his finances in order again. He did not know how he would handle the problem about his nights with the whore. He checked into the very hotel that he had sex with the prostitute.

He still had three days left on his vacation and decided he would spend those three days trying to find a buyer for his second car. He also made an application at the bank to remortgage his house.

He finally sold the car to a used car dealer and was paid $1,800 in cash for it all of which was in twenty dollar bills. That was $300 more than he had expected. He placed the money in an envelope that the car dealer gave to him as it would not fit in his wallet. He signed the title and gave the dealer a receipt.

He learned later that the Government was giving new car buyers a stimulus payment of $3,800 if the buyer turned in their old gas burners and bought a new "green" car as they called them. He was sure that the dealer would title that car and give it to a new car buyer who had no trade in.

In Josh's mind all looked as if he was on the road to solving his financial problems. He had $1,800 in cash to pay his delinquent credit card payments. His next step was to go to the bank and check on his application for a new mortgage.

When he arrived at the bank he was directed to a small office off the main lobby and the loan officer told

Josh that the bank could not re-mortgage the house for him because the current value of his house was less then he owed on the mortgage.

Josh's hopes for an answer to his problems had just been completely destroyed. He was further advised that his credit status had been downgraded because of the late payments on his credit cards and his mortgage.

He left the bank with his plans for recovery in shambles. He drove home and took the mail out of the mailbox. In the mail were two letters from creditors and a letter from his employer.

He opened the letter from his company and without reading it he saw the words "Our Company regrets to advise all of our employees" reading on he learned he was being discharged because his employer had been placed in bankruptcy. His company was a supplier of parts to General Motors. He was in a state of shock and was at a loss of what he could do now. He had lost Mary for certain. She had told him this may happen and he had ignored her warning.

When he recovered from his immediate shock, he got in his car and drove off uncertain of just where he was going. He stopped at a bar about 10 miles north of his home to have a drink in hopes that he could settle down and think about his troubles and come up with another approach.

He could not drink away his state of depression and the more he drank, the more upset he became and started telling others in the bar that he had lost his job, his home wasn't worth what he owed on it, and all of his troubles were caused by the damned Washington politicians.

He didn't mention his poor decision in buying an expensive boat and motor or his spending all of his savings to buy the boat. Instead he blamed all his troubles on the damn Democrats and the damn Republicans, throw them all out of office, he was yelling louder as the drinks kept coming.

He was getting drunker by the hour. He had attracted three other men to his table and they joined him in his exhortations and largely in the drinking.

One of the three was a hardware salesman and he complained that his sales were down almost 25% below the previous year. Another was a local house painter and the other was a mechanic who claimed that more people were repairing their cars and keeping them in good shape, He thought his job was secure. They never exchanged names. The three were soon trying to cheer Josh up and amuse the other bar customers at the same time.

One of them asked," Did you hear the one about three old men wearing hearing aids? The three were sitting on a park bench feeding the pigeons and the first one said its windy today, the second one said, It's not Wednesday its Thursday and the third one said. Yes I'm thirsty too, let's go get a beer."

Everyone laughed except Josh, all he could do was make a forced smile and said, "That's a good one - Hey bartender I'll have another beer too. I'm Thursday." Everyone was laughing again.

Did you hear the one about two blonds who were down by the river? No, someone yelled tell us about them. Well one of the blonds was on one side of the river and the other blond was on the other side of the river. One blond hollered across the river "How do I get across the river" and the second blond yelled back to her "you are already on the other side." Someone yelled I don't get that one, and the salesman, yelled back, "Stupid, they were on opposite sides of the river she was on the other side already."

Late in the evening, he told his drinking buddies that the next drinks were on him. He reached for his wallet and found it empty. He then placed his hand inside his coat pocket and withdrew a handful of twenty dollar bills from the envelope. He was having trouble placing them in his empty wallet after paying the bar tab for his treat and dropped them on the floor.

His drinking buddies did not see that he had taken the money from his coat pocket but helped him get the unused bills into his wallet. The bartender announced a last call and thirty minutes later the bar was preparing to close.

The drinking was over and one of the three men who had been setting at the table said his farewells and prepared to leave. The salesman helped Josh to his car and told the painter that Josh was in no shape to drive and that he would drive him home.

"What about your car?"

"I don't have a car here. I'll catch a city bus back to my hotel. This guy certainly can't drive."

"No, he sure can't. Glad that you will see he gets home OK. You take care. It's been fun."

The salesman asked Josh for his keys. Josh fumbled for the keys, and eventually found them and gave them to him. They left the bar's parking lot and Josh didn't give a thought to the fact that he had not told the driver where he lived or the fact that he was staying in a motel. He was just too drunk to realize where they were going. He passed out as soon as he was helped in the car.

Josh was driven to an access road through a wooded and heavily overgrown area where his drinking buddy pulled out a pistol and hit Josh on the side of the head and pushed him out of the car.

Josh fell bleeding and unconscious to the ground against the car. The salesman removed Josh's wallet from his rear pocket and threw it on the passenger seat of the car. He then pulled Josh away from the car so the door would close and after seeing that Josh was still unconscious, got back in the car and drove back out the dirt road to the highway.

He drove out onto the highway and sped off to make sure he was away from the area of his robbery.

After a few minutes he slowed down to check how much money was in the wallet. He reached for and picked up the wallet to remove the bills and in doing so failed to see a gasoline tanker truck making a turn directly in front of him. The truck collided with him head on and overturned spilling gasoline all over the truck's cab and the overturned automobile. There was an immediate large explosion and a huge fire ball.

As the car overturned, its passenger door was ripped off and some contents of the car were strewn on the ground and roadway including Josh's wallet. Both drivers were wearing seat belts and stayed in their vehicle as it burned.

After about 20 minutes with the traffic backed up for several miles in both directions the police, an ambulance, and several fire trucks arrived. It was too late to do anything but attempt to put what was left of the fire out and to clear a path to get the traffic moving again.

It had been burning for well over an hour before they could completely clear a path for the traffic to bypass the scene. As the fire was eventually extinguished and the traffic moving safely around the sight, they went on with their usual investigation and were clearing what debris there was on the highway when they found Josh's wallet on the side of the road with $180 cash in it.

They also recovered a baseball cap, some papers that had figures on it but no name or address on them as well as some mail addressed to Josh. The local newsmen were now on the scene taking pictures and interviewing the police, firemen, and the coroner who had been called to the scene.

They obtained Josh's name and address from

the police who had the wallet. After the police had confirmed from the tags on the car, that it was owned by Josh Merrill, the reporters began calling in their stories for their respective newspapers. Frank Spenser worked for the Midland newspaper and was at Mary's home when the police, a priest, and a neighbor arrived to comfort Mary when she was told of the accident and Josh's death. His article appeared on the front page of the Midland newspaper the next morning.

Josh woke up well after dawn and was still a little drunk. He had no idea where he was and suspected that he had been robbed during his passing out drunk, he remembered only leaving the bar with one of his drinking buddies.

He reached into his coat pocket, his car keys were gone, and so was his car but he found his envelope with the money from the sale of his car still there. He did not stop to count it.

So he had not been robbed as he suspected, but when he reached for his wallet and found that it was missing he realized that he had indeed been robbed, but luckily the robber had not checked his coat pockets where the big money was.

He remembered that he had used some of it to buy a round of drinks. Now he counted the money in the envelope and found that he still had $1,500. Damn it all, he thought, Mary will surely leave me or divorce me now. What kind of a fool am I? Did she wonder where he was and he wondered if she was still as mad as she was with him the day before. He thought she probably didn't care where he was. Damn it, I have lost $300 plus the dollars I had in my wallet in that bar.

Then he looked around and began to wonder just where he really was. He remembered nothing except leaving the bar with someone. Where was he and how did he get here, where was his car?

He was just not able to come up with any answers so he started walking out the long dirt road leading out of the wooded area. He soon came to the highway where there was a service station, and a small diner just down the highway at an intersection with a stop light. He walked down to the diner went in the diner's restroom and cleaned himself us best he could. Then he found a seat in a booth and ordered a breakfast and a cup of coffee. He needed some time to plan his return to his house and family. That was going to be a mighty difficult task. He then saw a newspaper rack near the cash register and got out of his seat to get one to read as he drank his coffee.

He opened the Midland newspaper and in bold headlines he read LOCAL MAN KILLED IN FIERY CRASH. He read on and found out that it was his car that had crashed into a gasoline tank truck and both Josh Merrill of Midland and the truck driver were reported as being killed.

Both drivers were completely burned when the many gallons of gasoline exploded. The article stated that the name of the truck driver had not yet been determined but Josh Merrill was identified by his wallet that was found on the ground near the accident scene and the tag on the car.

The vehicle was traced to Josh and he was further identified as such by a check of the motor vehicle department files using Josh's name found in the wallet. There was a question as how the wallet got out of Josh's pants but the police report surmised that Josh may have been looking for something in it and in doing that failed to see that the truck was approaching him in Josh's own lane. Why else would his wallet not be in his pocket?

However, It was officially determined, without question, that the truck hit the car and was at fault. The accident was the result of the truck being in the wrong lane on a curve.

Near the bottom of the news article it stated that Josh's widow had been contacted. She told them that Josh had not come home all night. She had intended to call the police and report him missing in the morning. She advised the police that Josh was depressed and she had just learned the today before that he had lost his job.

She was asked if Josh would be getting termination pay from his company as most discharged employees had received. She told them no, they told her yesterday that his company was in bankruptcy. Did she think that losing his job had anything to do with him having the accident? Did she know where he was going at that early hour in the morning?

She did not answer the questions but she did tell them that she did not know what she would do. She mentioned when asked, that Josh did have two life insurance policies on his life that he had bought years before to make sure that his children would have money for college. At least the children would have funds for college and that she would get by somehow.

The reporter continued asking her questions and asked if she would be suing the trucking company. She said "Please don't ask me such questions at this time. My children have lost their father and I have lost my husband. I have no idea what I will do."

Josh was totally sober after reading the story about his reported death, and ordered more coffee as he contemplated what he was or should do now. He thought about the two insurance policies he had bought, as Mary had told the reporters. He had forgotten about them, he may have been able to get needed cash from them. Each of those two policies was written on his life in the amount of $100,000. He had bought them when each child was born. It was intended to take care of them should he have an early death.

Josh had considered suicide before stopping at the bar after being told his mortgage could not be re mortgaged. Perhaps a few drinks would give him the courage to do that. Those policies will surely satisfy all of their current debts and would provide for the children as well as Mary. His financial problem had been answered. His death, as reported in the newspaper, was giving him the only answer to her problems he thought, his death.

I have been such a fool, I have lost everything that was dear to me and I have put them all into a miserable position. Mary is surely going to divorce him because of the whore situation. And the events of last night will surely be all she needs to do that if he was to go home. Her life is in total misery. Perhaps I should just disappear and let them be fixed for life with me out of the picture. I could disappear and start all over.

Yes, he decided that would certainly be a way of my getting out of debt and Mary Louise and the children would be fixed for life. That's the least that I can do for them now. Maybe I really can make a new start. He confirmed his decision and asked a trucker that was having breakfast in the diner at a table next to his for a lift to the next town North of Midland. The trucker agreed, "I'll take you all the way to the Canadian border if you wish. It will be nice to have someone to talk to."

He was dropped off at the bus depot in the next town where he purchased a one way ticket to Dallas Texas. The truck driver had told him that he looked as if he had just come off a drinking binge. Josh told him that was exactly what had happened. He was not used to drinking as much as he had last night and that he still had a hell of a hangover. That too was true.

After buying some casual clothes to replace his dirty suit and after getting a hair cut he waited in the public library to pass the time while he was waiting for the bus to arrive later that afternoon for the first leg of his trip to Dallas.

He didn't know why he chose Dallas, but it was far from his home in Midland, Michigan and that was all he wanted just now. Josh Merrill's family would soon be out of debt. He was a new man. His burdens were off his shoulders.

Mary and the children would be financially sound as soon as his insurance policies were paid. The kids would soon have their college funds back into a savings account. All he needed to do now was make plans for his own future.

Mary would probably remarry and the children would have parents to watch out for them. He was spared a divorce. Josh Merrill was dead. He was to become a born again new man.

But what he had to do now was to get a new identity very soon.

Chapter Two

Mary had received her checks from Josh's life insurance policies. She paid her mortgage in full and the credit cards were all canceled and paid in full. Four weeks after Josh had died; she received a call from the Marina Bay Boat Sales, in Florida and was told that they had sold Josh's boat. She received a check for $25,500, which she immediately put back into her children's savings account.

Her children were now assured of a college education. She applied for a job in the library and was given a job on the information desk and arrangements were approved that allowed her day to end at 4:00 each day so she could be at home when her children came home from school.

Mary's depression was slowly decreasing and her life as a widow was changing rapidly. The children no longer kept inquiring about their daddy. They had been told that their daddy had been killed in an auto accident. Mary was active in their school activities and had started to join her friends in some social events.

One of her old closest friends, Marge Newton, was now a single lady having been separated from her husband for over a year, and was waiting for a divorce hearing in a few weeks. Marge and Mary were a twosome at their church group activities or when playing cards with their old bridge club. Marge confided to Mary that she was hoping to find a new husband and that she was dating again. She asked Mary if she would be interested in double dating sometime. Her friend had a lot of single friends. Mary told her that she was not interested in dating at the present time.

When Josh arrived in Dallas, he knew that he had to get a new identity soon. He was quickly running out of cash. He could not provide any references such as a Social Security number or any past employer data and that made his job hunting very difficult. He decided that he had to obtain a new ID. He had read on the internet at the library just how ID's were being stolen and how many of them were obtained using a deceased person's name.

He scanned the newspapers at the library to see if he could find a deceased individual about his age and one that probably had a good credit score. On the third day of his search he found a possible name that he might be able to use.

The picture on the obituary that Josh found

interesting was of Joseph B. Miller. He had a very similar facial appearance as Josh and was just two years older than Josh. His obituary indicated that he had suffered a heart attack and was the owner of an automobile agency in Dallas.

Josh took note of all the names, listed in the obituary, their places of residence, and addresses were obtained for many of them. Using telephone books, he cross referenced the addresses with actual street addresses. He had everything that he needed but an actual credit card, a drivers license, and a social security number.

He rented a small apartment in Denton, Texas just north of Dallas to establish a mailing address. He then applied for a Texas driver's license as a new state resident and was issued one with no problem.

He called the local social security office in Dallas and told them he had lost his wallet and needed a new social security card. He was given the procedure for obtaining a new card, and was pleased that he had all the data on Joseph B Miller that he needed to get a new card. He had obtained all the answers he needed from the obituary.

He was told that his card would be mailed to his Denton address. He had everything he needed but a credit card, but within two weeks after he had opened an account at the Denton bank, he was sent an application to obtain one. He opened the account in the name of his new ID Joseph Miller and listed his occupation as self employed and added that he was the owner of an auto sales agency.

He was advised that the card had been approved and was surprised that he had been given a credit limit of $25,000. His new ID was working well. He was determined that he would never again let his balance approach anything near that amount. He wanted to start all over again by finding a job, and eventually finding a new wife. In the meantime, there were prostitutes. His task now was to find employment.

As he was searching for a place to apply for work, he passed an air force recruiting office in the local mall. He dropped in the office and entered into a conversation with the recruiter, telling him that he had lost his job and was wondering if a man of his age in the late 20's could still get into the service. When he told the recruiter that he was a mechanic, the recruiter told him that there was a need for mechanics and he was certain that he would qualify.

Josh though it over and came back the next day to make an official application. He had concluded that he could not find a better place to become a new individual. Most all of his living expense would be provided and he could gather a great background for employment after he left the service.

He was accepted into the air force and was assigned to the air base at Universal City, Texas for his training. After his training he was immediately assigned to specific training classes on airplane engines as well as air force land vehicles.

Within a few weeks he found himself enjoying working on the engines. It brought back memories of his past jobs as a mechanic in Midland. He made new friends and became a close friend of a fellow mechanic named Henry Hopkins, who like Josh had lost his job and joined the service so that he could provide for his family. Henry was married and was from Arkansas. He had one child a girl who was just 3 years old.

He told Josh that his girl was about to have her fourth birthday and that he was sorry that he was going to miss her birthday and wondered if Josh would help him find a gift for her.

He asked Josh if he was married and Josh told him "I was married, but my wife and I are divorced. I have two children a boy six years old and a girl who is almost four, almost the age as your daughter."

It had been several months since Josh last thought of his family and he immediately went into a bad state of remorse. He did miss them terribly and wondered just how they were doing. Had Mary got over his reported death? Was she starting to date other men? Was there a way that he could get the family back again? Did she love him enough to take him back?

Perhaps he could stay in touch with her whereabouts and when he left the service, contact her and convince her to come back to him and assume his new ID. She could become Mrs. Joseph Miller. Yes that would work.

But he had to make sure that she remained unmarried. If she married someone else that would cause problems. He had a sleepless night trying to think of how he could get the family back.

The next evening he was so excited about making this work out he went to a bar near the base to celebrate. He met a pretty young girl of no more than 21; who, he found out in short order, was a prostitute. Josh accepted her offer but he was thinking of Mary. This was his first time with a woman since he was last with Mary in Florida.

He went to a mall near the base with his new friend, Henry and they picked out a few gifts for Henry's little girl. They bought her a Barbie doll and a stuffed animal, a soft and cuddly little beagle puppy. Josh was tempted to buy something for his children but had second thoughts about that and decided that he would simply send Billy a birthday card next month on his birthday with some money inside. The gifts could come later as his plan to get them back was beginning to be finalized.

A few months later Mary opened her mail box and found a post card addressed to her that read "I hope that all is well with you and the children. I think of you every day. I love you." It was unsigned and had been mailed from Universal City, Texas.

Josh had written the card when he was depressed and thinking of Mary and the children. He missed them terribly. He felt he just had to make a contact with them even if he could not let it be known that it was him.

This was his way to get some relief from his sorrow.

She would not know who sent the card if he did not sign the card or use any kind of return address. He dropped the card in a mail box on the street corner on the way to a nearby bar. After he dropped the card in the street collection box, he regretted having done it. He had to be more careful and control his impulses to make contact with his family. He had a few drinks in the bar and soon left with a prostitute who he had met there several times before. On this night she had listened to his sobbing tale of how his wife was going to divorce him because he had had an affair with a girl just like her. He did not mention the other problems or that he had struck her in the face several times in the past when he had got mad.

On his way back to the base he remembered that it was just such an encounter as this that when Mary had threatened him with a divorce. Again he regretted having mailed the card. He was aware he had broken the law by assuming a false ID. He had to be careful. He had to get the family out of his mind.

Mary tried to think of anyone in Texas that she knew but, could not think of anyone. She mentioned the card to one of her co-workers who told her that it might be from someone in the Air Force, as there was an air base in Universal City and her husband got his training there. He was now a civilian.

Mary still could make no connection to anyone that would be in the service and certainly no one that would have sent such a personal card. The sender knew she had children, and had said he or she loved her. Only a very close friend would use the "I love you line." She knew no one at the moment who would be wishing her well. She assumed that one day someone would ask her if she got their card.

Josh completed his training and was transferred to the air base at Dover, Delaware where he was serving in a maintenance crew on the planes arriving from foreign bases. Their cargo was mostly with those killed in action. He saw the many flag draped caskets being unloaded from the incoming planes.

They were normally unloaded into hearses after dark from the planes far away from public view. His job was to service the incoming planes in preparation for their departure back overseas the next day. They normally were flying to and from Germany and he had asked the pilot about hopping a ride to Germany some time. The pilot assured him that could be arraigned and who Josh should contact for approval.

He made such a trip to Germany a few weeks later. In Germany, he thought of his son Billy, remembering that he had just had a birthday. He bought Billy a gift that he could mail from Germany. He knew that Billy would be impressed by having received a package from

Germany. He gave no thought at the time that he should forget the children. He could not forget them even if he tried. They were still embedded in his heart and memory.

Billy would like to tell his schoolmates that he had received a gift mailed from Germany. Back in his room waiting for the flight back to Dover the next day, he realized that he better not mail the parcel because his new ID may be discovered.

It would be easy to trace military records and it would probably be known that the mailer was in the service. He gave Billy's new Swiss multi blade knife, still in the box, to the son of a German lady who worked as a maintenance employee in the mortuary building on the base. At least he did make a little boy about Billy's age very happy.

He was uncomfortable on the return flight to Dover. His seat was in the cargo area along with a dozen or so flag draped caskets. He wondered if there had been a memorial service for him. Had anyone offered to make a eulogy for him? He smiled as he wondered if Mary had stood up and said he was a big Shit as she had once called him.

He was enjoying his work at the base.

A few weeks after his return from Germany, his new team co-mechanic, Norman Costa, mentioned that his son was having his twelfth birthday. He told Josh he had worked it out for his wife and son to come to Salisbury, Maryland where they would celebrate the birthday of their son with his wife's parents. They lived in Salisbury, Maryland. Salisbury was just a few miles south of Dover. No more than sixty miles he told Josh.

Norman had hoped that he could get leave for a day or two while they were in Salisbury to take his son to see the Atlantic ocean from Ocean City, Maryland, just East of Salisbury. His son had never seen an ocean before because he was born and still lived in Kansas. His grandparents always came to Kansas and he had never made a trip to see them before.

He asked Josh if he had any children and Josh told him that he had two children but he had not seen them in over two years because he and his wife were divorced and she had custody of the children. That is why he joined the air force. He had forgotten that he had put on his application that he was divorced and there were no children. He had to be more careful in what he said in the future.

That evening, Josh was mulling over his conversation with Norman, and realized that it had been well over a year since he left his family and he had assumed his new identify of Joseph B Miller. His son Billy had a birthday just last month. He wished that he had kept that Swiss knife he had bought him in Germany and gave away. He could send it to him if he had kept it. Again he had second thoughts about sending the gift. He decided to send him a birthday card.

That could not be traced to him. He missed his

family terribly and was well aware that he had to be careful in making any contact with them.

The urge to send Billy this gift overcame his fear of exposure. He could do so without drawing the truth of his disappearance. He would pick up a gift in Salisbury and mail it there.

Norman had agreed to accept Josh's offer to drive him down to Salisbury to visit with his wife and her parents. He told Norman that he would take Norman to Salisbury to see his wife and child so he could spend a two days with his family. He would do some shopping and go down to Chincoteague, Virginia to spend a day or two fishing out on the outer banks and he would pick up Norman in Salisbury for their trip back to the base. They could save having to rent two rental cars. That was an ideal arrangement and Norman agreed to the plan.

Josh Merrill had been dead for over a year now. He had been without family over that span of time and had been unable to shed his loneliness. Being around Norman's son, caused him to want to do something for his son Billy and only increased his obsession to get his family back once again.

On occasions, he had dated a few women who lived on the base and had often frequented bars where he could always find an available prostitute only to find out that his love for his family just could not be shaken. He was still in love with Mary and he was obsessed to find a way to get her back.

There just had to be a way to get his family back.

There had to be a way to do that without destroying the happiness he was certain they were enjoying, thanks to his life insurance policies.

He had to be careful and make his moves very carefully. He wrote the Midland Newspaper and subscribed to it, as Joe Miller. Mary Louise was probably happy with her security and would probably never want him again. But he was sure there must be a way. He was becoming more obsessed every day with the thought of their getting together again. It was on his mind every day. The newspaper used to run a column written by a Frank Spenser on local events, marriages, deaths, and his specialty human events. Perhaps that may give him information on Mary. When he had married Mary their wedding was announced in Frank's column as well as reports about Midland people who were vacationing in Florida.

Mary retrieved her mail as usual, from the box on the street in front of her home and saw an envelope that was addressed to her son, Billy. It was mailed from Delaware and postmarked at the Wilmington Delaware Sectional Center facility. She knew no one from Delaware and she was anxious to have Billy open it so she could see who had sent him a letter.

When she went into her house she called Billy and told him that he had a letter. Billy opened the letter and found a birthday card inside with a message that read "Billy, sorry that I missed your birthday but better late than never, I guess. It's hard to believe you are eight years old already. I miss seeing you. Hope your mother got you a birthday present. I will be sending you one in a few days." Again the letter failed to have a return address or a signature.

Mary wondered who would be sending Billy a birthday card and had her wondering just who knew Billy well enough to know his birth date and his exact age. Didn't anybody sign their names to letters anymore? Suddenly she remembered that she had received an unsigned letter from someone in Texas a month or so ago.

She was still mystified over that letter and wondered if they were from the same person. She had a restless night and wondered if the sender would indeed send Billy a present, as he said in the card. Perhaps they would not forget to sign their name or a return address this time.

She received her answer in a few days when she received a parcel addressed to Billy which had been mailed at Salisbury, Maryland.

Josh had driven Norman down to Salisbury and had dropped him off at Norman's parent's home.

In Salisbury, before he left for Virginia he went shopping for a present for his own son Billy as he had promised him in a letter earlier.

He remembered that Billy had always wanted his own fishing rod but at the time was way too young to handle one. He was now eight years old but Josh felt he was old enough to start playing with it. He had his own fishing rod and reel when he was about that age. Josh thought that he was at the right age to start fishing. He bought a tackle box, filled it with the usual fishing gear, a spinning reel, sinkers, lures, hooks, and line and placed two $20.00 bills in the tackle box with a note that read.

"I couldn't get you a fishing rod. It could not be easily mailed to you, so ask your mother, to buy you a nice one at the local sports store with the money in this box. Tell her to look for one at Henry's Sporting Goods Store on 33rd Street. They carry all the best brands. Get a good rod because they last a lifetime. Have fun and catch a whopper on Cat or Murphy Lakes. When I next see you, I will take you on an overnight fishing trip on Higgins Lake."

Again, there was no signature or return address. Mary was beginning to feel uneasy about this situation, and at work the next day she told the Librarian all the events to date and wondered how she could find out who was doing this. She told the librarian that the sender knew all about Billy, his birth date, names of local lakes and had even suggested a particular store to buy the rod. She had no idea who knew such facts about Billy or the area. He had to be very familiar with Midland.

The librarian told Mary that she didn't want to upset her, but that perhaps Billy was being set up by a pedophile. There seemed to be a lot of that anymore. She thought that Mary should talk with someone at the police station just to be sure. Mary had not given that a thought but immediately became hysterical.

Perhaps Elaine, the librarian, was correct, could that be a possibility. She guessed that if it was a pedophile, perhaps he was watching Billy right here in Midland. Maybe he had a job that required a lot of travel. That would account for the distant mailing spots.

She decided to get the police involved as Elaine had suggested. She ran to the libraries rear window looking over the back lot of the library. Billy was lining up his soldiers for an attack on those lined up a few feet away. "Billy" she yelled, "get your soldiers and come in here right away."

Billy did so. He often played in the back lot when school was out and he was required to wait for his mother to get off work. Sometimes his sister Nancy joined him, but she usually went directly home with her neighbor and close friend Marcia. Marcia was the daughter of Mary's closest friend and neighbor Dorothy Clark and Dorothy picked them up at the school. Then she remembered that one of the cards was addressed to her and not Billy. She decided to call the police anyway.

She called the police station and told them all the events to date and her new concern. The officer who took the call, Detective Robert Mitchell, told her that he would come to the library and take her statement if that suited her. He felt that it was important to do it immediately, as there had been several reports of problems with pedophiles recently.

Mary asked the librarian if that would be OK, and she agreed. She also offered Mary the use of her office for the interview.

Detective Mitchell arrived at the library in a matter of minutes, Mary was in tears when he arrived. Who could be doing this to her little boy? He took her statement and asked her if she had any idea who could be doing this? She replied that she had no one in mind.

The officer said that this sort of thing was not unusual especially after a woman loses her husband. Men looking to make friends with a widow often made their first contacts through the children. Did she have anyone who may have liked her before she had married Josh? Had she seen any strangers hanging around the area? Did she know any men who had lost their wife lately?

She replied to his questions "Not any that would know about Billy or who would do a thing such as this. Do you think that a pedophile could be involved? Will he hurt my boy?

Bob told her that pedophiles do not normally do anything other than to watch the children themselves. They work alone and would never give a written statement of their attraction to a boy. They normally just stay in the background and wait for an opening.

Being that all of his contacts were from such a

distant points; he didn't think that a pedophile could be involved; but he told her that just to be sure the police would be watching her house and around Billy's school.

Mary suggested that maybe it was a local pedophile that had a job which required a lot of travel, as she had thought earlier. Bob told her that if that were true it was different from steps pedophiles normally took.

He insisted that it was more likely someone who knew she was a widow, and was trying to make a good impression on her before he got up the courage to confront her. He added that was the answer on the vast majority of cases where the police are called in on.

He told her, one day soon he will face up to you and ask you if you got his mailings. He will then tell you how lonely he is and hope that the meeting will be the start of a new friendship.

The men involved in most of our cases that involve a widow, such as you, usually are men who have lost their own wives within the past several years. Another group is men who once had known the widow before her marriage.

It is almost always someone that has dated the widow in the past. Many are just too shy to come out and make a point to talk to the widow. "Do you know any of your old friends who may have lost their wife in the last year or so, or any unmarried men that had a crush on you in the past?"

"No not off hand" she replied. Bob's discussion

made Mary feel a little better. Her fear that it was Billy that someone was after now took a back burner and she felt more at ease.

Bob went on to tell her that widows are easy targets for all the weirdoes out there and that someone may be trying to get to her through her children. If he ever asks for money, even for something that you might be inclined to send him some, under no circumstances do not do that, until you clear it with us.

He went on to explain the reason why he asked her about any possible suitors was because he felt that perhaps a former suitor may be looking for an opportunity to renew a relationship with her. A large number of widows or widowers make contact with old suitors and many times they eventually get married.

My guess, he told her, would be that this person does a lot of traveling, because his contacts are from different places. He probably is afraid to contact you directly until he has gained your confidence in his actions. He has made no threats to you or to Billy. He really hasn't broken any law up to this point. I am rather confident that it is someone you really know. He plans you or Billy no harm.

"Can you think of any men, who are unmarried, or have ever made a pass or seriously liked you?" "You know you are a very attractive young lady and would be a great catch for any man." "Someone in your past would be my guess at the moment, if it is not a relative who just assumes you know who he or she is that is mailing the letters and gifts."

"I have no idea Bob, who that could possibly be." Mary did have several individuals in mind, but she was not about to tell Bob about them. One was married now and it surely would not be him. The other was a young man named Patrick O'Malley who she had dated years ago, who had never married but he and Mary were merely close friends and the two had been going out for dinner or the movies for several months now. The subject of a marriage was never considered. Pat had told her many times that he would never marry. He had also taken Mary's friend Marge to dinner many times.

Mary was in fact having dinner and a movie with him that very night.

"As I mentioned earlier we will place your home on a watch order and if you see a police car passing by at odd hours, don't get excited, if will be one of our officers keeping a watch for unusual activity in the area. At times they may be in unmarked cars and parked in the neighborhood. If you do see anyone parked near your house, give us a call anyway so we can determine if it is one of our men or not."

"Do not tell even your closest friends or neighbors what we are doing. If you do you may upset an action that we are taking."

"Keep me posted on any other letters or calls that you get or if any men are making contact with you. Do make sure to notify me if you get any more unsigned letters or any telephone calls. Most likely we just have an individual that assumes that you know who he is and it all will come to light soon."

Mary and Patrick were having dinner at Red Lobster and the reporter Frank Spenser saw them and he went to their table and talked with them several minutes telling Mary that he was happy to see her out again. Spenser was a close friend of Patrick's and kiddingly told him, "About time you settled down Pat Mary would be a great catch for you." Laughing and then he left for his own table without another word.

Pat told Mary. "He's always trying to find me a wife. I have told him a hundred or more times, that I am a confirmed bachelor. Perhaps he doesn't know that I am gay."

In his Thursday column, he wrote "Shades of a four leave clover, Patrick O'Malley, Midlands most confirmed bachelor, is on the loose. He was seen twice in the past few weeks having dinner with a lady. Is he about to forego his reputation as a bachelor for life? If so, he was seen having dinner with a beautiful and eligible widow, Mary Merrill. Mary lost her husband in a terrible fire a few years and would certainly make him a good catch. "

Josh read this article in the paper and was distressed to see that Mary was going out with another man. It was only a little over two years since he left. He did not know this Patrick O'Malley but he had to do something if he was going to get Mary and the children back when he could work out a way to do that. He had to get O'Malley out of the picture. His subscription to the Midland newspaper was paying off.

After a few weeks had past, The Midland newspaper had an article on the first page that read "A Midland man, Patrick O'Malley, age 32, was found shot to death at his home in Midland and the police have no suspects on who or why he was murdered. His wallet was found intact with a large sum of money in it. Mr. O'Malley was single, and his housekeeper stated that there did not appear to be anything missing in the house in so far as she could determine."

Mary called Bob Mitchell at the police station and told him that she did in fact have dinner with Patrick a few weeks ago and she was concerned that the person writing to her and her children may have been involved in the murder. Maybe he had read that stupid article in the paper about his having dinner with me. Bob told her that he had already come to that same conclusion and he had placed those possibilities in the O'Malley file.

When Josh returned to Dover AFB after having had a five day leave, he read the Midland paper and was pleased to read that the police had no suspects in O'Malley's murder and were requesting leads from O'Malley's friends. He was not pleased to read that the police were investigating reports of Patrick's homosexuality. That could perhaps slant the reason for the murder towards a sexual thing. But damn, he thought, I could have saved a week of my leave if I had known he was a homosexual. He probably would not have married Mary in spite of what that reporter had written about his having dinner with her and the possibility of his marrying her.

Over the next six months the letters and cards to Mary and the children increased. It was rare for a week to go by without an unsigned letter or a small gift being received. As she had been asked to do, she reported each instance to Bob. He made a habit of coming to her house after every call. The police were very interested in these letters to Mary because of Bob's report stating that there may be a connection to the O'Malley murder.

Mary's neighbor, Dorothy, told her one day when Bob had called and said that he was coming over, "You know Mary I think Bob is the one sending you all those letters just to spend a few hours with you."

"I swear Dorothy I think you are determined to get Bob and me together. It's all business these letters are driving me crazy. Bob really is a nice guy though isn't he? He does comfort me when we get together."

"There you go; see what I mean, Mary you have a suitor on your hands and you love it. It won't be long before he asks you out to dinner. Just you wait and see."

It was only a few days before another package was delivered to Mary. This one was again mailed from the Wilmington Delaware Mail Facility. That facility handles all of the mail to and from the state's post offices where mail sorting machines are located.

This parcel was addressed to Mary's daughter Nancy. It was the first item that was addressed directly to Nancy. It had a card enclosed that read "Gosh Nancy, I am so busy, I forgot your last birthday just as I almost forgot Billy's last year – enjoy this beautiful little doll I saw in the mall and I thought of you when I saw it. Have a happy birthday even if it is late. I am sorry. I must mark my calendar so it won't happen again. Tell your mother I think you are lucky to have a mother as nice as yours. She is certainly a wonderful mother isn't she?" As in the past, no signature or return address were on the parcel.

Mary called Detective Mitchell and told him, "Bob, we just got another parcel." Bob asked her if there was an address or name on this one and she told him "No; but this one is addressed to my daughter Nancy. It is the first one to her. Is he after my daughter now?"

"No. His plan is evidently changing. I bet you will be the next to get a nice present from him and then he will make his move. He wants you very badly. Save the wrapping on this package for me and I will be right over to pick it up. We are getting quite a file. I think we may have a "Loony" on our hands. It's late and I haven't had dinner yet, if you haven't eaten, how about if we discuss the situation over dinner? The dinner will be on the city?" With no hesitation Mary e agreed.

Mary called her neighbor, Dorothy, to see if she could watch the children while she had dinner with the detective. Her neighbor agreed to babysit the children and kiddingly told her. "Well it's about time you went out with him Mary, I told you he had more than police work on his mind and that he would soon invite you out to dinner. Remember? Josh has been dead now for about two years isn't it?"

Mary replied, "Yes, just two years next month, but this is a meeting with Detective Mitchell, I got another parcel today. This one was addressed to Nancy. It's all business."

"Oh, that's good news if it was addressed to Nancy, then that would eliminate a pedophile. A pedophile wouldn't be after both sexes, would he?"

"Dorothy, I swear, you keep me scared to death, I don't know."

"I'm sorry Mary, I don't mean to scare you I just felt that a pedophile could have been involved up to now, but because he sent this parcel to Nancy and as I have been led to believe, pedophiles usually direct their attention to children of the same sex and not to both sexes. I think now that the mailer is most likely not a pedophile. That should be good news. Perhaps one of your close relatives or friends is the one mailing the parcels. Can't you think hard and come up with some names?"

"No, I have tried and tried. I simply cannot come up with a single person. What scares me now is that in each note in the parcels, he seems to makes a reference to me and he seems to be trying to get my attention."

"Mr. Mitchell told you that was his plan a long time

ago, remember? Why do you think that he wants you now Mary? Has he made any requests to contact you? And if not, why would he keep dragging this thing on and on? Why doesn't he just come out and ask you? He has spent a lot of money sending those letters and gifts?"

"Well he said in one note he said that he loved me. Another one said that I was a wonderful mother, and in all three parcels he mentions me somewhere in the notes."

Bob arrived in a few minutes and examined the parcel carefully and told her, "Mary save all these messages and especially the wrappers. We may need them for writing comparisons or evidence in the future." "I think I'm in the mood for some seafood. Want to try Red Lobster?"

"That sounds great to me; I haven't been in a seafood restaurant since Josh died."

In the restaurant during dinner she asked, "Bob were you ever married?" He replied that he had never been married. "I'm surprised you certainly appear to be a nice catch for some young lady. You are quite handsome you know."

"Thanks for the flattery Mary I think most women must think differently. I can't remember the last time I had dinner with such a pretty lady. When I got out of high school, I went right into the military because I was unsure of just what I wanted to do. I just never found the right girl, and after I was discharged from the Army after a tour in Iraq, I joined the city Police force.

"It seems I was just too preoccupied with my work, I guess. Let's not talk about me, why hasn't a nice attractive lady like you found another man yet?. I think by these letters you have someone may be thinking of you with that in mind."

"Bob, I have two children to take care of and they keep me too busy to think about anything else. I must admit that I do get lonely at times but I am still a little depressed over the loss of Josh and with the burden of bringing up my children on my shoulders. I don't think I am ready for another man just yet."

"What kind of a husband was Josh? Was he good to you and the children?"

"Bob, I could never have found a more devoted husband or a father for my children; but, he was always trying to pretend he was more than he was. He was very jealous of many of his friend's that were successful and fought to keep up with them. The week before he was killed he struck me in the face and caused my nose to bleed. He had done that perhaps five or six times before. He had a very bad temper and was easily riled up."

"At a party one New Years eve, one of his friends came up to me and kissed me. Everyone was kissing everybody, you know how that goes. When Josh saw the guy kiss me he came over and hit that guy in the face and knocked him to the floor. I was very embarrassed and he apologized to the guy after I told him that he was out of line. He was very jealous of me and that wasn't the first time that he had lost control of himself. When Josh was angry I was truly scared of him. He had hit me many times."

"Why didn't you tell us Mary? I always thought Josh was a devoted father and the kind of man every woman would love to have. In fact I was always envious of him."

"Bob as I told you, he was truly devoted to the children and to me for that matter. He just had a terrible temper when he didn't get his way or when things went wrong. He couldn't handle it. I knew that he always hated himself when he lost control and because of the children I always managed to forgive him."

"The night before he was killed, I argued with him about our large debt. He got very angry and he hit me the hardest that he had ever hit me before. My nose bled for a half hour or more. I sent him out of the house and told him that I had had enough. I had made up my mind that I was going to file for a divorce. I told him that and he went out slamming the door behind him. I meant every word I said and I know that he knew that I intended to do that. That was the last thing that I ever told him."

"When he died, he left me with a great debt to pay but lucky for me and the children, when each of his children was born, he took out a large insurance policy on his life to assure their future in the event that he would die."

"Like I said he was a devoted father and husband. He gave me and the children everything that we could possibly have ever wanted and most often, he gave gifts that we could not afford. Just before he died, when we were in Florida he bought a very expensive boat and motor just so he could keep pace with our friends down there."

"That is the main reason for our having such a debt. That pretty much describes what kind of a man he was. We were actually at the point of a separation the week before he was killed; I had not spoken to him for several days. If it had not been for those insurance policies, I would have lost everything."

"To tell you the truth Bob, I often wondered if he had that accident purposely to resolve our financial problems. I have a feeling that he would have done that for us. Especially when he was in such a frame of mind after I told him that I was going to divorce him."

Bob admitted, "Well, I can tell you now, that we had considered suicide at the station the night he was killed and we gave that suspicion a lot of attention at the time for sure, but the driver of that gasoline tanker was clearly proven at fault, because he was definitely driving in the wrong lane, when he collided with Josh's car. It was assumed that the truck driver had fallen asleep. I knew about the boat and his debt. I understand that Josh had the boat up for sale. Was that sale ever finalized?"

"Yes, but it was sold at a huge loss after he died.

Those funds were a great help at the time. That alone paid all of our creditors except our mortgage and his credit card balance was reduced to the point that we could have handled them. It hurts me now when I first thought that he may have committed suicide and was at least trying to solve our financial problems. He was extremely distraught when he lost his job. I failed to work with him when he was trying to do something to solve our problems."

"He died thinking that I had given up on him and remembering the terrible things I said to him the day before he died. I am positive that we were heading for a divorce. Bob, am I just putting a lot of worry on myself over these letters and packages, or is it just my imagination that something is wrong?"

"Bob, promise me that you will keep this conversation between the two of us confidential. I would hate for it to get around our friends or to my children."

"Between us only, it would certainly serve no purpose. He's out of the picture now, I promise to do that."

She was told that her feelings were exactly what everyone whose marriage was in trouble, always wondered.

"That is because they always have the feeling that they may have been the one at fault, regardless of the actual reason but almost always his investigations and experience in such cases as this the marriages are usually doomed to fail any way.

"You are right in being concerned about the present situation but let us do the worrying for you. It is our job to protect you and the children. Besides I am determined to get to the bottom of all this." He also had the urge to protect them.

"Mary did you note that in his last two contacts you were mentioned fondly in both of them. Even in your first letter remember he told Billy to tell his mother to buy him a fishing rod, and in this one he mentioned that he thought you were a wonderful person. And in one letter he actually said that he loved you if I recall correctly without looking at my notes."

"I think that his real interest in all this is you. Why else would he say you were a wonderful person or that he loved you? Most of his contacts so far seem to have been sent around birthdays. I wager the next contact will be on your birthday. Since he started mailing these gifts, have you had a birthday, anniversary or something?"

"No, and I don't recall him saying right out that he loved me. Did he do that? My birthday was in May, on the 17th, just before Billy's, which is June 22, he missed mine."

Bob said, "That adds even more strength to my thoughts on this matter. I think that there's a chance that it was your birthday that really brought you or your family to his attention. He certainly knows a lot about your family."

"We need to do some serious thinking. Just who do you know that would know the birth dates of your children? I am sure that these messages are coming from a relative or from someone that has or had access to a genealogy record or such records."

"Tell me; have you or Josh ever had a genealogy record of any kind done in the past? Did you ever receive birthday gifts or cards from any relatives?"

"Yes, we have prepared a genealogy of our families but we have never done anything with it. We never printed the findings. It is all on my computer. We always got gifts from the children's grandparents. But you can forget them Bob, because they both sent cards to the children this year and both visited with us and brought their gifts. They surely wouldn't mail separate gifts."

"Yes, I know I have already contacted both of the children's grandparents."

"Oh Bob, I wish you hadn't done that, I already asked them if they had sent the children another parcel, and they both said that they had not done so. I hope that you did not scare them."

"No, Mary, they both told me that you had talked to them already, and I told them you had asked me to help find who had mailed the parcels and that I had thought that it was mailed by one of their grandparents."

"In fact they both thanked me for helping you out and I think that your mother thought that the two of us had something going as she was telling me how nice a girl you were. She was hoping that you would find another man soon. Kiddingly, I told her that I was available."

"You didn't really say that did you Bob?"

"I sure did, I am single and available remember?"

"I am still of the opinion that you are being harassed without the senders actually realizing what stress he is causing you. I think that soon he will be making a move to meet you with the hope of a marriage. Can you think of anyone that may have such a wish? It could be someone that is married and separated awaiting a divorce. There has to be a reason for his moving so slowly."

"No, I know of no one that ever sent them gifts in the past, some sent cards but never any gifts."

"Are you sure that you have told me about anyone with whom you may have had any kind of a relationship, or about any person that may have had feelings for you prior or after your marriage to Josh? I would bet that would be a strong suspect." With that question asked, Mary smiled at him and said, "Well my neighbor Dorothy said that it was probably you so that you had an excuse to keep seeing me."

"Gosh I didn't think of that maybe some of our troopers think that way too." Seriously Mary, I think we have a weirdo out there and he is disturbed. His writings and gifts are not something that a sane man would do. I think that he is obsessed with getting to you. A sane man would have made contact with you personally by now, or there is a reason that he can't make his move on you yet. Are you positive Mary that you have told me about all of your past friends? You must think hard, this guy may be dangerous."

On that statement, Mary started crying and with heavy tears in her eyes, and her hands over her face she said, "Yes I do have someone in mind now that may fit. Bob promise me that you will not put what I am about to tell you into any official documents on this matter."

"Mary I will promise you that; but you must remember that I am a policeman and I can't hide anything that may have a bearing on the case. I must include it if it becomes a part of the answer as to who is doing this and then only if it winds up in a criminal charge. Even then, I will see that it does not get into any records unless it is absolutely necessary, fair enough?"

"Yes, I feel I can trust you Bob. Understand; what I am about to tell you, is a very personal matter and I really hate to tell anyone." Mary hung her head and started to cry again. "It is not only an embarrassment to me Bob but again please understand that serious damage may fall on my son Billy, if it was ever made public."

"I will understand Mary."

"Thanks." Still weeping and hiding her face from Bob she started her story. "Before I married Josh, I was dating a guy named Edward Stein. Ed was from our town and he later moved to Delaware. Oh dear Bob, I just remembered one of those packages came from Delaware!"

"Yes, I just made note of that as you were telling me

about him. I remember Ed well. He once tried getting on our police force but didn't make it. Seems he had something in his past and left town without taking his final trials. I never followed up on that or understood why. Go on with your story please."

"Bob, do you really have to have any more information about Ed, this is very embarrassing?"

"Yes, we do need to go on Mary. This may well be just what we need to settle this mystery."

"OK, here goes, and please do not hold what I am about to tell you against me. I have never revealed this to anyone, not my family, my priest, doctor or even to Josh, especially, not to Josh."

"Ed and I had been dating for some time and at a time I was also dating Josh. Ed told me that his family was moving to Delaware and that he would be going with them. He also said that hat he had accepted a job in Delaware and that he would be leaving at the end of the month for Delaware."

Hiding her face from Bob she said, "That because of our thoughts of possibly not seeing one another again and that we were secretly engaged to be married we did some passionate kissing and hugging and that in the end resulted in our making love. We made love. It was the first time we had ever done that and I was a virgin. He told me that he was a virgin too, but I rather doubt that. A few weeks later I discovered that I was pregnant. I told Ed that I was pregnant and told him that we had to get married before he left for Delaware. I would go with him. Ed refused to marry me and told me that he would pay for an abortion."

"Bob, I am from a Catholic family, and I just would not think about having an abortion. Ed dropped me like a hot potato. I had also been dating Josh for over a month. We were attracted to each other but we had never had sexual relations, although Josh had wanted to and we came close on several occasions."

"After Ed's refusal to marry me, I went out on a date with Josh, and without his realizing what I was doing, I made sure that he would try to convince me to made love on this date. This was also the first time with Josh. I told Josh a week or so later that I was pregnant and we were soon married. That's it Bob; my secret over these years, Billy was not Josh's child, and as far as I know, Josh never questioned that. I heard from Ed only once after that and told him that I had married Josh. He congratulated me and went on to explain that his family would have objected to his marrying outside his faith and that is why he refused to marry me."

"Ed was Jewish and he told me that he was going to marry a Jewish girl whose parents owned a clothing store in Newark, Delaware. He or I never mentioned my pregnancy during that call. I never heard from Ed again. Oh why, did I tell you this Bob, Ed had no way of knowing the children's birthdays or names."

"Mary if you will look at those messages, the mailer never mentioned any date. He said only that he was sorry that he had missed Billy's birthday. Ed would know the month that the child should have been born, so if he waited to send the message after the month Billy was to be born he would leave the impression, that he knew the exact date. Regarding the note in Nancy's parcel that would not hold true unless someone told him that you had another child. Do you know of anyone who may have told him that you had a second child and also knew you?"

"There were many mutual friends Bob, but I have no idea who would have done that."

"Mary, any of those friends of yours could have given him their names and birth months. There are also many other ways to get that information. I still believe that the mailer is using the children's gifts to get close to you. We now have something to start working on. I wish that you had told me of this sooner. Ed Stein may well be the one we are looking for."

"He is now my prime suspect. We need to do some more follow up work on this. Do you have an address for Ed?"

"No."

"Do you know where he lived in Delaware?"

"No, but one of our old friends, I can't remember who, told me that he had married a girl of his faith in Wilmington Delaware because Ed was Jewish. I told her that I knew that."

"Ah ha, that may give us some address or other information that may help us. It certainly gives us a reason he wants to get back with you. Who told you that? We can check the court house for marriage licenses etc. I will start some inquiries tomorrow. Let's celebrate, by having a lobster. Do you like lobster?"

"Sure do, I love it." Seeing tears in her eyes he took her hand squeezed it slightly and said, "Don't feel sorry or embarrassed about our conversation, I'm sure we will get to the bottom of this soon. And this will truly remain our little secret. I really think we have a possible suspect to check out now. I have a good idea. How about you and I going over to the Midland Elks lodge, have a drink or two and dance away the hurt you have just now?"

She forced a smile and agreed. "Thanks Bob, I am so happy that you are so interested in this case."

"It's my job Mary."

"Don't you take what my mother told you about me needing a husband as the truth, she wants me married so she can spoil another grandchild that's the main reason."

"Oh, I was hoping she was right." Bob replied smiling.

"You were hoping that I was looking for a new husband or someone to give her another grandson?"

"Both. I enjoy your company and for the first time in my life, I think that I have found just the girl that I have been looking for. I think that I am truly in love with you."

"Even after what I just told you?"

"That is not a problem for me."

After dinner they went to the Elk's Lodge, where they danced to all the slow songs. They were soon dancing with Mary's head resting on Bob's shoulder, and he holding her close to his chest.

She whispered in his ear said "Guess what? I think that I am falling in love too. I do need a man in my life. You have been so patient with me and you do comfort me so."

After the dance ended they left the lodge and Bob drove to Mary's house. They sat in the car for about an hour discussing their pleasure in having found one another. That perhaps they should have dinner again and the subject that bought them together was not mentioned.

They kissed for the first time and the second time and countess other times.

When Mary went in the house Dorothy was there to open the door smiling. "I knew it I knew it. Why didn't you invite him in?"

"Not on the first date Dorothy."

Chapter Three

Mary called Bob the following day after her evening out at the Midland Elks lodge and told Bob, "I have another letter from him and I think you will be interested in this one."

"I'll be right over, are you home or at the library?"

"I'm home, I just got off work." This was the first letter addressed to her personally that she had received from her unknown harasser. It was a long printed letter that was entirely typed in lower case. The guy was certainly not a typist she thought. Before all his contacts were placed inside gift parcels or letters addressed to the children. She thought that he has finally made contact directly to me, just as Bob predicted.

She looked for a return address and as usual there was none. There was no signature at the end of the letter. It had been mailed in a foreign country ten days earlier, and the foreign stamps indicated that it had been mailed from Paris, France.

The letter stated that he was in Paris on vacation after a business trip to Germany and he had taken a side trip to Paris. He wrote that he remembered her telling him years ago that she would love to have gone there, and he thought of that when he landed in Paris.

Mary had always wanted to go to Paris, but who knew that, With Ed as the suspect now, she wondered if she had told Ed of that wish. She must try to remember who she had ever told about her desire to go there should it not be Ed. She was sure that she had told countless people of that dream. The message went on to say that he wished she was there to see the sights with him.

He confessed again that he had always loved her and wished that she was there by his side, so he could renew their love.

When Bob arrived and started to read the message he told Mary, "Did you note that he used the words renew their love? This indicates that he did at one time love you."

Mary did not answer the question because Bob was already continuing to read the message. The writer wrote that he had been shopping and bought her a special gift and she would be receiving it in a few weeks. When she got it she would realize just how much he cared for her and wanted her to be aware that he would see to it that she had many gifts of that sort if they could just get together again.

He went on to write, "I must find a way for us to get together soon." He did not offer an explanation or reason why he could not do it just now.

Bob said "Maybe he and his wife are separated. Or his family is still opposed to any relationship out of their faith. At any rate we will soon have answers to all the questions we have regarding Ed. Surely you must recall anyone who had loved you. Can you think of anyone else other then Ed Stein?'

Mary's best recollection of men that had ever told her that they loved her was Josh, Ed, and of course just last night Bob. She said "Oh yes, a drunk had told me that at a New Year's eve party in Florida when he tried to kiss me at midnight, He didn't even know who I was. He loved everybody. What a slush he was."

"Also try to think of anyone who may have loved you, not actually sexually, just anyone who may have had a crush on you?"

"Bob, I have never had sex with anyone but those two Ed and Josh. You must believe me. I can't recall anyone that had a serious crush on me. If they did, I was unaware of it."

"I have a serious crush on you Mary, do you know that?"

Bob had already contacted the State Police in Delaware and a file had been found on an accident report in which Ed Stein's wife was killed. The address of the Steins at that time was listed in the report and indicated that he live in Stanton, Delaware. Ed was an employee of the du Pont Company in Delaware at their engineering building near Newark. He must have been an engineer as that is where the companies engineering facility is located. His wife, Elaina, who was killed in the accident, was a nurse at the Veterans Hospital in Elsmere Delaware. There were no children. There were no charges filed against Edward Stein, they were struck by a DUI driving at a high rate of speed on Interstate I-95 just south of Stanton.

Bob had requested that the Delaware State police check to see if Ed was still living at that address. He was. The telephone book listed him still at that address and his telephone number was recorded in Bob's notes.

Later that night Bob called the number given to him and Ed himself answered the phone. Bob asked, "I am trying to locate a man named Joshua Merrill and that someone had advised me that you may have once known of his whereabouts."

"Why are you looking for him? I haven't seen him in a very long time?"

"Josh owes our company branch in Clearwater, Florida, a large amount of money for storage charges on a boat we had in storage for him and we want his permission to sell the boat for him. He will have money coming to him even after we collect what's due us. I bet he has forgotten that he left the boat with us." Bob had fabricated the lie using information that May had given him. He was hoping that Ed was unaware that the boat had been sold several years ago and Mary already had the funds. "Would you know where he lives now?"

There was a hesitation and Ed replied, "I really knew little about him except he was from my old home town in Michigan, but I did read in my old hometown newspaper, that he had been killed in an auto accident. That's probably the reason he hasn't called for the boat. I don't know where he lived in the city but I think his wife still resides there. Perhaps she can help you, her name is Mary Merrill. I'm sure that she would like to know she has some money coming. She may need it now that her husband is dead."

Bob made a note for himself that Ed had read of Josh's death in his home town newspaper. That could be the source of the children's names he used in his parcels. Bob asked, "What was the name of the town you were from?"

"It was where I used to live years ago. A town in Michigan called Midland. I am sure that his widow still lives there, as an old friend of mine told me that she was working at the library there." After a few seconds of hesitation he added "but I don't know her home address off hand."

Bob made a note that there was a hesitation before he mentioned that he did not know her home address. Was Ed thinking that he may be providing information? Could he be aware that he was being questioned about his past connection to Mary? Did he have a reason for the hesitation? At any rate Ed told Bob."That's all I know, I have to run, hope you find the information you are seeking. Goodbye."

Bob thanked Ed for the help and hung up.

He then contacted by phone the Wilmington police officer that had given him the information earlier that day and told him that Ed may have been involved in a case of harassment that he was working on, and asked if they could find out if Ed had remarried after the death of his wife, or if he was seeing other women. Had he been traveling across the United States?

Was there any reason that they could find that would have placed him in Universal City, Texas about a year or two ago?" And remembering that Mary had just told him that she had received a parcel from Paris, he added the question, had he travelled to Europe over the past year?

The officer said that he would look into all that and be back in touch with Bob in a day or two. He added that Ed had no complaints or record in their files. His passport may reveal the answers to some of Bob's questions. He would seek that passport information from the proper Government authority.

Later that afternoon, Mary called Bob and told him, "You won't believe this but I just got a package addressed to me and it contains a most beautiful dinner ring, and a note. I think it is a diamond. It wasn't even insured."

Bob asked, "What does the note say?"

"It says that - well let me read it to you - My dear

Mary Louise, I have finally got enough nerve to send you the gift that I bought for you some time ago when I was in Paris. I am indeed sorry for all the problems that you have been faced with since I last saw you.

"I had planned to buy you this special gift many months ago because I wanted you to know that I was aware of your problem. I am working on a way to make myself known to you. I hope you will wear this dinner ring and consider it as an engagement ring, until such time as I present you with a real engagement ring."

"I didn't want to rush back into your life until I had convinced you of my love for both the children and yourself. I sent gifts to the children many months ago in hopes they would develop a favorable opinion of me and welcome me when we do meet in the future after I work out some of my own problems."

"I just learned this week that you are seeing Bob Mitchell of the Midland Police and that it appeared you two were becoming attracted to each other. Mary you are my love and my life, please don't get involved with him."

"That is why I sent you this ring. I want you to know how much I love you and I want you. Please do not marry him and tell him - I will not give you up without a fight. My love for you will not allow him to share your bed. That is why I am making this move at this time. I am determined to have you and no one will be allowed to get in my way."

"Bob, This man is insane. Pease come over as soon

as you can, I am very scared and concerned about this note. It has a threat in it. Can't you come over right away?"

"Yes, Mary, I will be there in a few minutes. If he made a threat in the letter that will completely change the complexity of the case. He will have broken a law. A federal law no less, using the U.S. Mails to threaten someone makes it a federal case, I will be right over."

When Bob arrived, Mary was at the door waiting for him and crying profusely. She grabbed Bob and told him, "Bob, how could he know that I was falling in love with you? I do love you. You have been my sole support since all this started. I'm afraid for you now. Did you hear me when I read his threat? Take a good look at this ring. That center diamond musts be at least two carats. If it is real, his intentions must be real also."

"Yes, Mary it certainly looks real to me but we can have a jeweler look at it to make sure. We have enough now to call in the FBI to assist us on this matter and if my suspicions are correct, they will be of valuable assistance in our locating the suspect."

"Bob, I can't figure out how he could possibly know about our seeing each other. There must be someone local feeding him information."

"It looks like that Mary, but there are always ways to obtain information without one knowing what they are doing. I told you from the beginning months ago, that you were the target and not the children remember?"

"Yes, I remember that. Now I am afraid for you."

"Please don't worry about me; I know we will pin him down sooner than you think."

The next day, they went to the jewelers and had the ring appraised. They were told the ring was indeed gold with a perfect white diamond of slightly over 2 carats, and the side gems that circled the diamond were blue sapphires. He estimated the ring had an insurable value of at least $5,500. "Someone must love you a lot." the jeweler told Mary.

Mary said," Wow, that's the sort of thing that only Josh would have done."

"The reality of the case has changed Mary. He has gone beyond the stage of harassment and is now threatening harm. He has a warped mind it seems, and he has definitely set his sights on having you. I say warped mind because, if he were normal, all he would have had to do was confront you in person and ask for your hand and get your yes or no."

"Why doesn't he come right out and ask you if you will marry him? I think he was or is not free to do that. I suspect that he is probably waiting for a divorce or something, but I just got word that Ed's wife was killed in an auto accident. So he is now free to make a move for you."

"Well Bob, I can tell you he won't succeed in getting a yes from me. All the love I have is for you. I do fear that he will hurt you. He sounds like he is just crazy enough to try."

"Don't worry about that Mary, I know how to

protect myself, now that I am all but positive that we are on the right track, our next step is to find him before he gets into more trouble than he is in now. We have experts on finding people once we know who we are looking for. I talked with our Chief and he suggested because of our relationship, that I get off the case, but I convinced him that I should stay on it. Reluctantly, he allowed me to stay on the case."

"Do you remember that I told you last week that I was planning a special little vacation for us to put all of this behind us for a few days? I hope that this new letter has not changed your mind? Do you think that Dorothy, your neighbor could take care of your children so we can slip away for the weekend?"

"Perhaps, what do you have in mind?"

"Well it would start off with a dinner and wine at Alfonso's Friday night, then on to the theater to see Guys and Dolls. Saturday morning we would drive down to the lake and rent a small sail boat. I haven't done any sailing in years, but I know we will have fun. I will have you home Sunday so you can rest up. I plan to keep you busy. I have seen Guys and Dolls several times, but I do like the music in it. Have you ever seen it?"

She replied that she had seen it years ago, and that she too enjoyed it. "Then do we have a date Mary?"

"I haven't been away overnight from my house and children for years now, and except for our night at the Elks, and a few dinners with friends that's about it. I do think I need a break. I'd love to spend the weekend with you. I do love you so. Yes, we have a date. I'll go with you. I'll ask Dorothy about babysitting; but, I know she will because she has been pushing me for weeks to go out with you again."

Bob picked Mary up promptly at 4:30. She had put on an evening dress for the first time in many years. She had bought a new dress for the occasion, and Bob, had on a shirt and tie and a sports jacket. Mary had never seen him with a shirt and tie before. He was not armed. She was sure that he had weapons in the trunk of his car as she had seen them before.

"My, don't you look nice and attractive tonight?"

"Not near as nice and beautiful as you are."

After Bob loaded her overnight bag and small suitcase they said their goodbyes to Dorothy and the children and left on their first weekend together.

Mary said, "Bob is there a chance that Ed or whoever is writing me knows we are together tonight. I still fear his threat? By the way, I forgot to tell you Dorothy told me that she had a call a week ago from a man that said he was looking for me and that he had heard that you and I were planning on getting married, and he wanted to know if we had set a date. He told her that he wanted to send us a wedding present."

"He told Dorothy he lived in Europe and didn't want to miss the wedding. She told him that we were not engaged, to her knowledge, but that she felt we would probably get married soon because we were dating now.

Do you think that is how Ed or whoever is doing this got the information about us seeing each other?"

"Mary, you have to start letting us know of everything that you hear. That very well may have been the guy and how he got the information about us. He probably thinks we have a tap on your telephone calls, and called your neighbor instead. He's evidently a smart guy. Insane but possessed. He seems to be obsessed to have you at all cost. I don't know anyone that lives in Europe. He absolutely does not know where we will be over the weekend. I have told no one."

"Let's promise not to mention that subject again while we are together this weekend. We are supposed to be resting and having fun, remember, just the two of us."

They arrived at the hotel and checked in. Bob checked in as Mr. and Mrs. Robert Mitchell. Mary noticed that when he registered in, and smiled. They quickly opened their suit cases, placed the few items of clothing that they brought in the dresser drawers and Mary refreshed her hair.

Sitting on the edge of the double bed Bob told Mary, "I can't believe how all of this has worked out. I regret your having all of your troubles that brought us together, but in a way, I am sure glad we did get together. I think I fell in love with you on the day that I took your statement in the library."

"I became attracted to you that same day, but I realized that I was falling for you the first night we had dinner and you held my hand to comfort me. I can't recall Josh ever holding my hand to comfort me especially when I was so distraught with our financial position. I was so comfortable when you did that. But I think, that I knew I was in love with you after, I told you about Ed and Billy."

"I was really happy that I had finally mentioned that to someone. I had been carrying that secret all the years I was with Josh. You accepted my story and I felt relieved after you told me that it would remain a secret that we both would hold. I would hate to give Billy a problem at this stage of his life."

Bob leaned over towards her and they embraced and they kissed passionately for several minutes until Bob, whispered in her car, "We better go have dinner so we won't be late for the theater. If we don't leave now, I am afraid that we will miss both dinner and the theater."

At the restaurant, Mary told him, "Bob I think this will be the loveliest day of my life."

He replied that the day was not over yet, and that he had a lot more planned to make it a memorable day for both of them. She smiled at him and said, "Can I bet on that?"

"You can, just wait and see." They both ordered lobster tails and the waiter brought a bottle of chilled wine to their table without a word from Bob. Bob had already ordered that service as well as the choice corner table that offered the most privacy.

It was Friday night and on Friday evenings the

restaurant had a lone singer who played dinner music as their guests ate. He sang and played nothing but soft music.

In the midst, of the dinner, Bob, raised his arm so that the singer could see him, and without a word being said the singer approached their table and started singing "Misty" which brought tears to Mary's eyes.

Bob truly had everything set up for it to be a memorable evening. Bob seeing Mary in tears reached for her hand and took out an engagement ring box with his other hand and presented it to Mary, while the singer continued with his version of Misty. Bob looked at Mary and said softly, "Will you marry me sweetheart?"

Mary nodded yes and with tears running down her cheek, looked him in the eyes and answered, "Yes, yes, I will."

Hearing that, the singer stopped singing to announce to all in the dining room, He said very softly over his mike, "Ladies and Gentlemen – He said, pointing to Bob, will you and then pointing to Mary said "Misty said yes she would. Congratulations! The song Misty works every time."

All the diners applauded until Bob stood up and said, "Thank you" and went to Mary's side of the booth and pulled her up to himself and gently kissed her for everyone to see. The diners all applauded again and the singer switched to a hand clapping version of "Let the Good Times Roll" to everyone's repeated applause.

On their way out of the restaurant and to the tune of "Always", all in hearing distance wished them good luck - that was wonderful - God bless you both - and other words of praise.

They arrived at the theater on time and had hardly sat down before the lights dimmed. Bob whispered to her, "I do hope you like the theater. It is my favorite thing to do."

Later she said,"I think that actress who is playing the part of Adelaide is extremely good."

"Yes, she sure is, and the guy playing Frank Sinatra's old part of Nathan is pretty darn good too."

The lady in front of her turned her head just far enough that they both knew they needed to stop talking, even if they were whispering. They smiled at each other and held hands until intermission.

At intermission Bob asked Mary if she wanted anything from the concession and she said that she did not, but excused herself and told Bob, "I think I better take a trip to the ladies room before the show begins again."

Bob said, "Good idea I will go up front with you. Are you sure that you don't want anything, a candy bar, or anything?"

"No, I am still full, that lobster was delicious but filling."

Bob really didn't want anything and did not need a trip to the men's room. He had suddenly remembered without telling Mary, that they had received a threat and he wanted to make sure all was OK.

They returned to their seats and Bob realized that there was no way that anyone knew where they were or where they had been. He sat back and they enjoyed the show.

After the show Bob asked her if she wanted to go have a cup of coffee, and she said, "No. I just want to be with you alone so we can talk. I have a million questions for you."

"OK, then we will go back to the hotel. But remember no questions tonight on any of those questions that I know you want to ask me. Only pleasant questions for us tonight OK."

"Yes. I agree, I want to know more about your family, I don't even know if you are Catholic, Jewish, or an Atheist."

"I can assure you I am not an atheist. My father was a minister of the Methodist Church, and I have a brother that is following him in that career. I remember that you told me that you were Catholic."

"I did? When did I tell you that?"

"When you were telling me about Ed Stein, you told me that he was Jewish and you were Catholic."

"Oh, yes I remember now."

"Here's the hotel Honey, they will be sending a bottle of chilled wine up to our room, and we can sit back and talk as long as you want. I'll even tell you all of my little secrets if you insist."

"That's only fair, you already know about mine." Mary said, "You know it's been a busy day, I would like to take a shower and get comfortable. Then we would have all night to talk."

In their room now, "That's a great idea Mary, but I better warn you, I'm not going to let you keep me in conversation all night. I have a few other things we can do to make this a night one we will always remember."

"Yes, and I have an idea of just what you have in mind." They both laughed.

There was a knock on the door and Bob opened it. It was the wine that Bob had told Mary would be delivered to the room. He tipped the hotel waiter and the waiter opened the wine and poured them both a glass half full.

They drank their wine and Bob said, "I better get my shower first."

He took his pajamas and a finger length robe out of the dresser drawer and walked across the room where Mary was sitting and took her in his arms, pulled her close to his chest and kissed her passionately.

She pushed him away and told him, laughingly, "Go take your shower."

When he returned to the bedroom Mary was already in her nightgown, and she slipped by him to take her shower. Bob thought that she would never get out of the shower. He turned on the television and was happy to find that they had the music channels. He scrolled up and down the different channels and found just the one he was hoping for.

It was a music channel that played easy listening music and he stopped. They were playing "Always." Mary yelled out from behind the dressing screen off the bathroom, "Keep that channel Bob. I love that song."

The aroma from the dressing area was drifting into the bedroom just as she entered the bedroom dressed in a short black night gown. Bob took one look at her kissed her again and turned off most of the lights. He had already poured them each a small glass of wine.

They sipped on the wine while sitting up in the bed listening to the music and Bob reached over and turned off the rest of the lights. The conversation stopped.

The lights were turned on again in about an hour and they put their robes on.

Mary told Bob all about her family. She was born in the state of Virginia, in a little town named Floyd. It was great town to have grown up in. She knew everyone in town, all 150 of them.

Her father worked for the National Park Service, he was a Park Ranger. Her mother met her father when she got a job on the Blue Ridge Parkway and was assigned to the National Park's Welcome Center on the Parkway. The Blue Ridge Parkway was actually only a little more than its name implied, a parkway. It connects the Great Smoky Mountain National Park and the Skyline Drive of the Shenandoah National Park.

They were both full time career employees and were

now retired and live in Myrtle Beach, South Carolina after 35 years service. They still live there and her dad plays golf three days a week.

They both do volunteer work for the local hospital. She had one brother, Carl, who was two years older than she was. He was killed in Vietnam. He was never married as he went to Vietnam shortly after he graduated from high school. Her parents have never got over that war.

Mary said, "They are still angry that the soldiers that fought there were not afforded the support or admiration of the people of the U.S. and its politicians that is poured out to our veterans of other wars."

Mary told him that she went to college and got a degree in anthropology. When she got out of college she went to South Dakota and had wanted to join her parents in the National Park Service but her heart was set on being able to find work that consisted of research on dinosaurs.

She found such a job with Michigan State University in their anthropology Department. She went on several "digs", found some bones, but soon found that it was a hard and dirty job that required little knowledge. She considered herself a laborer to the professors, rather than an associate. She quit.

She moved to Michigan permanently to accept a teaching job at Midland. That is where she met both Ed and Josh. Bob knew the rest of her story. "OK, Bob now let's hear your story. I'm anxious to learn of your secrets you mentioned earlier."

Bob said, "Well maybe we will get to the secrets later, but first I'll start with my family as you did. My father, as I previously told you is a minister in the Methodist Church and my mother is a high school music teacher. Of course she also led the choirs at most of my father's churches. Some of his churches already had a Minister of Music when dad was transferred to other churches, but she most always found a job in the schools in those towns."

"My mother had a degree in Education with a major in music. She met my dad when he was appointed the minister of her Methodist church, in her home town of Peru, Indiana. I have one brother, Charles he followed in dad's footsteps and is now an ordained minister in his first church over in Minnesota. I don't know just why, but I knew that I was just not cut out for a life in the ministry. I was the black sheep of the family I suppose. My parents are now living in Boise, Idaho where he still has a church."

"The children of a minister have a difficult time in their childhood, especially with kids of their own age. They treated us as if we were the minister. They would not let us in on dirty jokes, and even apologized to us when they said a curse word. Girls had little to do with us. They surely didn't want to get involved with a religious freak.

I never had a steady girl in all my high school years.

In fact, I had never really kissed a girl in my life until I went into the military. Oh, I think I did give a girl a peck on the cheek once when I was about 13 or 14 and she slapped me when I touched her breast."

"You have probably seen or heard about the movie, The 40 Year Old Virgin, well that was me but I was 21 years old. OK. That is one of my secrets I mentioned to you.

"I was a virgin until I went in the military and a few of us recruits found a couple prostitutes in a bar near the base in North Carolina and that cost me $25.00 to get rid of that Virgin title. "

"Once I lost the title, I found it rather easy to increase my score. When I was shipped to Iraq there was no time for women, in spite of what you may have read or heard. Most of my duty in the military was in investigations, or in MP duty. It was this training that landed me my job with the Midland Police. They were looking for a detective and I met all their requirements and that took me to you."

"In case you are interested you just increased my score by one and let's see -- yes it's now at eight. Five with prostitutes and the other three with pickups in bars, but they were not whores but just girls looking for a good time. I'm sure that will increase at least by one more before morning maybe by two. But this time it was with someone I love. A first for me"

Mary said, "I hope so." Bob again turned off the lights.

It was just a little after one o'clock and Bob's score was now at 9. They finished their bottle of wine and Mary asked, "OK, now what's your other secret?"

"Well that was one of them. I was a virgin until I went in the military and the second was I made it all the way with a prostitute and she was actually my number one. Do you have any secrets other than the one I know about?"

"Yes, I do Bob, when I married Josh my score as you refer to it was only two. Ed and Josh were one and two. There were never any others. Tell me again what you have lined up for tomorrow I think you said we were going out on a sailboat at the lake."

"Yes, first we will have breakfast here in the hotel and then head for the lake. I have rented a sailboat to sail over to the island in the lake near the North shore where there is a lovely old and quaint diner and we will have lunch. I have made no plans for Saturday night. I thought that we could just stay here in the hotel, go down to the bar off the lounge have a few drinks, and sit around down there or in the room here and discuss plans for our marriage. Or if you wish we could take in a movie."

"That sounds great to me but I would prefer that we just stay in the hotel and watch a movie on TV instead of going out to a movie theater. I want to spend as much time as I can with you."

"I was hoping that you would say that."

"The rest of your plan sounds wonderful and looks

like fun. Bob we haven't discussed a wedding date yet. Do you have any date in mind?"

"Tomorrow morning would suit me fine. Maybe we could find a ship's captains to marry us." he laughed, and then added, "As soon as you want sweetheart. You set the date and I will schedule a week or so off."

"Not before two or three months have gone by Bob, I don't want you to think I pulled another job on you like I did with Josh."

"Oh no way Mary, I know better than that, I love you and I want to announce our marriage to my parents before that. My mother will be so happy. That's all she talks about when I see her."

"Sometimes I get the feeling that she thinks I might be gay. My brother's wife can't have children for some reason. I don't know why, and mom wants grand children so bad. Our two kids will make her a happy woman."

"Well, I can vouch to her that you most certainly are not gay. Perhaps a little over sexed, but certainly not gay. If we have a child someday, I bet your mother will be happier still."

"I know that she will love them all. She will make your children a grandmother."

"How about three weeks from tonight, and by the way, I know everywhere you have been and everyone that has approached you over the last four months. Remember the station has your every move under surveillance."

"Just kidding Mary, let's do it soon please. By the way I noticed yesterday at dinner, that you had not worn that beautiful dinner ring you got in the mail."

"No and you never will see me wear it. I thought about throwing it in the trash, but I have decided that I will sell it and put the money into the children's savings funds for Billy and Nancy. "A good idea Mary, would you consider having my father marry us?"

"That would be great - what a wonderful thing to do. It's getting late we will be too sleepy in the morning to go sailing tomorrow."

"Yes it's time to go to bed again but I got a feeling my score will soon be in the double digits before morning." He turned off the lights once again."

The lights remained off and she whispered to Bob, "Well you finally got to ten. A score of three in one night, I would never have believed that possible."

The next morning they had a big breakfast at the hotel and drove to the lake where their rental sailboat was at the dock and waiting for them.

Mary said "It's been a long time since I was last on a boat and I have never been on a sailboat. I hope you know how to do it. I sure don't."

He said that he could handle it; he went out sailing almost every two or three weeks in the summer months.

Sure enough he had them up to the north shore of the lake in less than an hour. He dropped an anchor and said I love this spot. There's nothing on shore to distract from the beauty of the lake and the surrounding forest. I come up here often, just to watch the birds. "There's a nesting area right over there and when the birds are here and mating it is a busy spot and a sight to see."

"Are they are as busy as we were last night?' She asked.

"Yes, he laughed, but not as busy as I plan to be between now and tomorrow morning before we leave. I want to do something now that I used to always think about when I was here alone enjoying the view and tranquility of the area."

"What was that Bob?".

"Go swimming in the nude." he said. "Take off your swimsuit and let's give it a try."

He stood up, dropped his bathing trunks to the floor and jumped overboard. Mary laughed as she took off her bikini bathing suit and joined him. Their score soon was increased by one. An awkward task, but it was accomplished when they swam to an area that was shallow enough that their feet could stand on the bottom.

Mary was laughing and Bob asked her what she was giggling about. She said, "If we ever get to go on one of those cruise ships out of Florida, I hope that we don't get picked to be one of the couples selected for the marriage game."

"One of the questions always asked is "What was the most unusual place that you ever made whoopee? I would hate to tell them in very cold water with an occasional boat passing by and fish nibbling at my toes." They both laughed. Then Bob added "I guess I would have to tell them that also, but with the fish nibbling at my little worm."

They both laughed.

They spent a hour or so swimming and playing like teenagers in the water before they got back in the boat, dressed, and pulled anchor. They sailed up to the diner and had cheeseburgers, fries, and a beer which they consumed at a table on the open porch with a beautiful view of the lake.

A couple who arrived at the diner on another sailboat joined them. They were friends of Bob. Frank Spenser worked for the local newspaper. His wife, Martha noticed the engagement ring that Bob had given Mary the previous evening, and the friends offered them their congratulations and then asked if a date had been set for the wedding. Frank said. "Well I guess my column will back up my earlier prediction on you two."

Bob said "I don't know the calendar date but it will be on a Friday night three weeks from yesterday, is that right Mary?"

Mary said "That's right it's Friday the 28th.

Frank said, "Well that will certainly end a lot of speculation. Everyone in City Hall and in the town that knows you two, have been predicting that event for over a month. Some were even offering bets that it would never happen and stated that Bob was a confirmed bachelor. In school Bob, if you will remember, you were voted as the class "Classmate most likely to remain a bachelor for life. How did you convert him Mary?"

Bob said, "Mary don't you tell him it will be in the newspaper."

After enjoying their conversation, they decided to see who could get back to the boat rental docks the quickest. Bob and Mary lost because Mary knew nothing about what to do to help Bob. And Martha was an old hand, an excellent crew member, and had participated in many regattas that were held on the lake.

They arrived back at the hotel just in time to have a shower, and be at the restaurant when it opened for dinner. After dinner, they took a walk around the block and went in and out of almost every store. Mary bought a tee shirt for each of her children that had printed on the front "ROSE LAKE". Bob bought a plastic model of a police car kit for Billy, and a 1000 piece puzzle for Nancy that when finished would be a beautiful aerial view of Rose Lake and the surrounding small camping areas.

He pointed out on the picture where he and Mary had gone skinny dipping. They both smiled.

They returned to their room, showered together, and got in their pajamas to watch the news when there was a knock on the door. The waiter brought in another bottle of wine in a cooler.

"Bob you think of everything. This has been a wonderful trip. You have everything arranged ahead of time. You think of everything. I love you so much. You are everything that I could ever want of a husband."

He turned off the lights and at 3:30 a.m. a new record had been set, counting the one in the lake it was now four in one day.

Mary said, "Well done Bob, but that's the end of the competition until we get married or again on a vacation away from the children."

Two weeks later Mary called Bob and told him that they were lucky. She didn't know why not; but she wasn't pregnant. Bob told her, "I wouldn't care if you were."

"Bob, I do love you so."

It was a week after Mary and Bob had set the date for their wedding. The Midland Daily, where Bob's friend Frank worked carried a weekly humorist column that Bob called a gossip column.

This Thursday's issue contained an item of interest to Bob. It read "Police Chief, Tony Valdata, had submitted his resignation after 25 years as Chief and the grapevine has him going to Florida. Congratulations Chief, we hate to see you go, but we do wish you well. Chief Valdata's resignation and retirement were approved, at a special meeting of the City Council on Wednesday night. Congratulations Chief Herles. Assistant Chief, Remo Herles was appointed our new Chief at the same meeting."

The next paragraph read "Speaking of congratulations and our men in blue, Detective Bob Mitchell, will marry Mary Louise Merrill on the 28th of this month. Mary is employed at the Midland Library. Mary is the libraries Information clerk. Mary lost her husband Josh, in a fiery vehicle accident three years ago leaving two children. Congratulations Bob and Mary. Mary's two children will give their mother away at the wedding – How about that?"

It was a beautiful wedding. Most of the Midland police officers and staff attended the wedding and were in full dress uniform. It was a breathtaking sight.

Bob's dad performed the wedding and his brother read a Bible verse that brought everyone's attention to the purpose of a marriage to bear children to populate the world, and their pledge made to each that they were bound to care for the other for as long as they lived and until death would they part.

Mary had agreed to a wedding outside her Catholic faith. Her lifelong priest was in attendance as were most of her catholic friends.

Everything went exactly as planned until Billy attempted to hand the minister the wedding ring, he dropped it and it rolled away with Billy chasing after it. When he finally caught up with it he handed it to the preacher as he had been instructed and said out loud, "Sorry about that Mom - it slipped right out of my hand." And Nancy responded by saying, "I told you to let me do that that Mommy I knew he would mess up everything." Everyone giggled even the minister had a smile on his face as he took the ring.

Bob and Mary left for a vacation in Mexico following a reception at the church's fellowship hall. They had not disclosed to anyone where they were going to spend their honeymoon.

When asked Bob, simply told them, "mostly in bed."

Chapter Four

When Bob and Mary returned to Midland after two weeks In Mexico, Mary called the post office to have them deliver the mail that had been held while they were in Mexico.

As soon as Bob arrived at the station for work, the officer on the desk told him. "Mr. Mitchell, you had a call yesterday from Wilmington, Delaware. Officer Jack Short there asked that you call him as soon as you came in today." Bob called Wilmington and asked for Officer Short and when they were connected. Officer Short told him, "Bob, we checked out Edward Stein as you requested and we did find some information that may help your case, Mr. Stein was in Paris just six weeks ago."

"He was actually on company business and we confirmed that with his employer; but the reason I called you instead of just sending the findings to you by fax was because Edward Stein was murdered last night in the parking lot where he worked."

Bob interrupted him and said, "You have got to be kidding."

"No, I'm not -I think we need to get together on this case Bob, because we have no clue as to who did this. He was not robbed and it looks like it was an intended murder. Perhaps your case may give us a lead as to why or who could have done this."

"If you can arrange things, I would like to fly out to Midland next Wednesday so we can look into the possibility that they may be connected. Would that date suit you? And could you have a patrol car pick me up at the airport? I will fax the flight numbers etc, if you agree to sit down with me."

Bob told him, "Yes, I was certain that they were related, but now I am not sure - I am anxious to meet with you. I will pick you up at the airport personally, because I would like to discuss several items with you before we meet officially, where every word we say will be placed in the transcript. Send me your flight number and when you arrive contact Bill Wilson in Security at the airport. You can use one of the red phones behind your incoming airline's boarding desk. They will see to it that we get together without a hassle. I'm glad that you will be joining me in this case. By the way have you made a search of Mr. Stein's residence yet?"

"We will be making a search as soon as we get the

Judge's permission and we will have that today. Is there anything in particular that I should be looking for?"

"Yes, I would be interested in any credit cards invoices he may have received that reveal any unusually large charges especially when he was in Paris. I'm looking for any large jewelry purchases, and any letters addressed to him that have return addresses. Any telephone numbers in his address book that has a Midland Michigan area code or a name of Mary Merrill in the book. If you find anything of interest I will certainly fly back East and join you in a more extensive search. Did you find any evidence that he was seeing any women?"

"No, to that last question, but we have already started an extensive investigation now that we have a murder on our hands."

"I will go over the entire file when you get here. Do you have any witnesses to your murder?"

"We have only one witness at this time, a woman who worked with Mr. Stein. She worked in the same building as Stein but not in the same office. She did not know him personally. All she could tell us was that she heard what sounded like a shot."

"She told us that when she turned around to see where the noise came from, all she saw was a white van; she thought it was a KIA, and she saw some type of insignia on the driver's jacket. She thought it may have been a policeman or security guard's uniform. I certainly hope it was not a police officer."

"She said he was speeding out of the parking lot and

she assumed that it was a policeman chasing someone. She said she was absolutely certain that he was wearing some kind of uniform. She thought it was blue but she was not sure." "I'm sure that you are working on that right?" "Sure we are. Our Internal Affairs are hoping that it was not a police uniform." The witness repeated most of what she told us. Their report said she thought it was a policeman and she thought that the policeman was speeding out of the lot to catch whoever fired the shot. His uniform was blue or light grey in color. Our officers wear light blue uniforms. By the way, the car was not a patrol car - Just a white van as I mentioned a while ago."

"I definitely would like to talk to that witness, so I am sure that I will fly back to Wilmington with you."

Bob did not tell Mary that Ed had been murdered on the telephone when he called to tell him he was on his way home.

When he first got home from work he told her that Ed was no longer a suspect and that Ed had been murdered in Wilmington, Delaware.

"Ed murdered Bob, by whom? Why was he murdered? Do they have his murderer?"

"We don't know yet Mary, but this really raises a lot of questions in your case. Was Ed your harasser or not? If he was; who and why was he murdered? We are working on it and I have a meeting set up with my counterpart in Delaware and of course the FBI is on the case also". He added, "I am rather certain now that it was not Ed that was writing to you and I am also certain who the guilty party is."

"Who, Bob, please tell me?"

Bob said, "Mary, please listen to me for a few minutes. No questions until I get finished. OK? When you mentioned that the ring he sent to you as something Josh would have done I gave that a lot of thought."

I have something to tell that I have suspected for some time now. I have been working and following up on another case at the station that I have not told you about because, up to this point, it was only a theory that I had with the possibility that may lead to your mystery man. I have a theory that the man may indeed connect. I think it is Josh himself."

"Josh how can that be Josh is dead? But please do go on"

"After the accident with the gasoline truck, I think that I told you this before; but anyway, there was suspicion that Josh had indeed committed suicide, but everything at the time pointed to that not being the case. It was proven by the investigators that the accident was the fault of the truck driver and not Josh. A witness to the accident also confirmed that the truck was clearly in the wrong lane, and the investigation at the scene indicated that to be true. The insurance company also investigated the accident and they too were convinced that it was an accident. As you know they closed their case and paid you the claims."

"But, let's get back to my theory, and it is only a theory Mary".

"About three weeks ago just before we went to Mexico, we received a missing persons report on a salesman out of Ohio. This man had called his home from Midland and said that he was moving on to Detroit and that the next day and he would call home when he got there. "

"While we on our honeymoon, the office found that his call from Midland was made the very night Josh was reported killed. It caught my attention when I saw that date. The salesman has not been heard from since that call. We had filed that case as unresolved because we found no evidence that could place the man anywhere in the Midland area other than the reported telephone call he made to his home. "

"He was on the road visiting hardware stores and could have been going anywhere but he said he was going to Detroit and we let it go at that. There was no lead for us to begin a search for him and we turned the case over to Detroit. We did contact his employer for a list of possible stops."

"We contacted all of them and found no trace of the guy. He had not been in any of their stores."

"But when the feature story of the missing man appeared in the local newspaper, we had a call from a Midland man who said that the salesman was in Midland and that he was drinking at The Midland Pub with him and two other men. The Midland Pub is on the same road where the accident occurred."

"He stated that he knew neither of the men but they had sat together for hours and were drinking pretty heavy. He said he saw the salesman leave with the other man who also was at their table. He recognized the picture of the missing man that was published in the newspaper and was certain that it was the missing salesman, but he did not know the other guy but he was drunk and in a sorry state of affairs. He said the other man kept talking about losing his job, politics and his other problems and he was trying to drink his sorrows away. He was very drunk at nights end when they all left the bar. He said that was the last time he had seen either of them. But he was sure that one of them was the missing salesman. He did not know who the younger guy was. I read this report on my return to work, and started thinking that these dates and reports were possibly connected with Josh".

"After I got your first call about getting parcels from someone who was so knowledgeable about your family, I was convinced that the case was a simple case of family misunderstandings. I made no connection to Josh. The vast majority of our missing cases are just that."

"But, at that time we had no reason to question the accident report and no one put the two cases together. It was only after you stated that sending you a valuable ring was something that Josh would have done, I began thinking and I finally put the two cases together looking for the possibility that it could possibly have been the missing salesman and not Josh that was burned up in the accident."

"We reopened both cases and did an extensive search of the wooded area near the scene of the accident to see if by chance Josh had been thrown from the car. We found nothing."

"I also read in the accident report that Josh's wallet was found at the scene and it contained less than $200 but we had also learned that Josh had been paid almost $2,000, in cash, for his other car just that day."

"I just could not put the two cases together or figure out what happened to Josh or the other $1,800."

"If he was in the car, as the guy who called us and told us why was there only one person in the car at the crash? I began wondering what had happened to Josh or the other man."

"The thought came to me that perhaps Josh had been robbed by the salesman. But why was there only about $200 in his wallet?" So I just thought the robbery theory was wrong. Josh was dead, but I still wondered if the man had robbed him and then abandoned Josh and drove off in Josh's car leaving Josh somewhere dead after killing him or to sober up after he was long gone."

"The wallet found at the scene flashed what I thought was critical to the case. It was apparently thrown from the car when it was struck by the tanker truck. It must not have been in a man's pant pocket. During the time following the accident the department contacted the used car dealer who had bought Josh's old car and he told them that Josh was paid $1,800 for the car and that after he gave Josh the money, Josh asked for an envelope to put the money in and that he was certain that Josh put that envelope in his jacket pocket. They were checking that as you had told the police that he had sold a car. The dealer told us the stack of twenties was too thick to put in his wallet. He had just got two packs of $1,000 in twenties from the bank, and he used those two packs of twenties to pay Josh."

"So now I had a reasonable explanation as why there was only $200 in Josh's wallet. The rest of the money was in Josh's jacket inside pocket."

"My only problem with this theory was what happened to the salesman's own vehicle. Was it still at the bar? But as I suspected he was using a rental car, and it was determined that his car had been checked in to the rental firm two days, before he was reported missing.

"Salesmen often check in their rentals at various cities, to save daily rental charges if they have multiple contacts to be made in the same city over several days." 'They find using a taxi cheaper then daily rental charges and they can make money on their per diem. The rental firm said that he was to pick up another car in about 4 days but he never came back."

"We then contacted the informant, the house painter in the bar again and he confirmed to us the fact that the other guy) was too drunk to drive and that perhaps the salesman drove him home. "I told him that the salesman did not have a car there. I showed him a picture of Josh and asked if the man in the picture could have been the other guy. He looked at it for several minutes and finally he said he just couldn't say."

"He only recognized the salesman for sure because he had an odd shaped mustache and sideburns, but all he remembered about the other guy was that he was so intoxicated he never really got that good a look at him. But he did think that his hair was much shorter."

We then did a checkup on the salesman and found that he had in the past been arrested for stealing funds from a drunk and served time in jail." With that information we dug into the informant's story. Mary said "Bob that picture I gave you was from a time before he got his promotion. He had his long hair cut short just before he went for his interview."

"Mary, I know all of this sounds farfetched, but I think that there is a possibility that it is all true and that Josh is possibly alive. I think he was thinking that it was a chance for him to start all over again, and happy that his financial problems would be taken care of with the insurance money."

"Now that you mention all this, Bob I noticed that in this letter I have right here he wrote my name as Mary Louise, Josh was the only person that I can recall, that always called me by my full name Mary Louise and I thought of that when I read Mary Louise in the letter"

"If this is truly Josh, why doesn't he let me know that he is alive." That's easy, Mary he knows that he would be arrested for faking his death and sued for restitution by the insurance companies. He would be right back where he was trying to escape from them, and he wanted his family to be happy."

"If this is all true where is he now Bob, and how can we get him to turn himself in?"

"That's the real question now Mary, He has gone beyond the stage of merely disappearing. I think he has a new identity now and has become obsessed with the fact that he cannot get back to his prior self and his family."

"I suspect that he will soon try to get you to join him in his new Identity. He just doesn't want to give up his family and as he said in the letter he will fight to keep it as it was. He probably is thinking of ways for you and the children to join him under new identities away from Michigan."

"Well, I can tell you Bob, he won't succeed in doing that. He has not changed one bit. That ring he sent to me is proof of that. He was always trying to prove himself with things beyond his means."

"I love you Bob, and the children love you as well. All the love I once had for Bob has vanished. I now fear that he will hurt you Bob. He has a terrible temper and acts without thinking of the consequences at times. If all this is true, what will be the legal status of our marriage?" "Don't worry about that Mary, I know how to protect myself, now that I am all but positive that we are on the right track, our next step is to find him before he gets into more trouble than he is in now. As I said before, we have experts on finding people once we know who we are looking for. As far as our marriage goes there will not be a problem. Josh was pronounced dead after the accident. Any judge will declare Josh's marriage to you at an end."

Bob told Mary that the FBI would soon be questioning her about the case that might give them just enough information to help them in their search for whoever is threatening you. It may turn out that Josh is not the one, but in a short time we will have that answer.

"Please tell the FBI team everything you can think of Mary. I have already told them what I know about the case."

"Do I have to tell them about Billy?"

"No Mary unless they ask you, Ed is now out of the picture and all they will want to know is things that will help them locate the guy making your life miserable or the cause of Ed's being murdered."

He told Mary, "Now that Ed is most likely off the list, they could concentrate on others. They would most likely start in Texas where her very first letter was mailed. Then they would be checking Delaware and Maryland. Perhaps even Paris. He told her that the FBI had mentioned that there was an air base in Universal

City, Texas and the murderer was seen with some kind of uniform on."

"Wait a minute Mary, I just thought of something. It may be the answer as to where our suspect is."

"Where Bob, please tell me." Mary asked.

"Later Mary, I think that a serviceman, one in the air force is our man. I have to get to the station right away and get together with the FBI guys. I hope they are still there. I'll see you later this afternoon and explain everything to you– please don't worry. I think we have a good start in locating this nut and it will prove it wasn't Ed at all."

Bob left in a rush. At the police station, Bob met with the FBI team leader Agent Calio, and told him a witness in Delaware had said that the man she saw in the parking lot where Ed had been murdered was in a blue or grey uniform. "I'm betting that uniform was of an airman. I think that our suspect may be or has been in the air force. Is there an airbase in Wilmington?"

Agent Calio injected, "There's a big one in Dover, Delaware. That's where all the dead soldiers are sent from the wars over seas."

Bob said, "Hey - that fits in with a theory I have on this case. Mary has received letters from both Texas, and Delaware and the most recent one was from Delaware.

"If my theory is correct perhaps Mary's stalker went into the service to hide with a new ID in Universal City. Mary's first letter was mailed in Universal City.

At that time she was asked if she knew anyone in the air force. She knew of no one in the air force and all of her friends said the same. Her second letter was mailed in Delaware, possibly at the Dover air base."

"I'm betting that her husband Josh did not die in that crash and went into the Air Force to hide."

Agent Wilkerson replied." "Basically we are already working on that Bob. We already had come to the possibility that the suspect may have been in the service when we were told about Universal City. We came to that possibility when a witness to Mr. Stein's murder claimed that the killer had on a blue uniform. Then we put together the places of mailings in your reports and the air bases in Texas and Delaware and came up with that as a possibility."

Mary arrived home from work and got her mail, and saw a letter addressed to her. She knew it was another letter from the same person. Without opening it she called Bob at the police station.

"Bob, I have another letter, I'm afraid to open it. This letter was just mailed two days ago. It can't be from Ed because Ed was dead when it was mailed. Will this crazy man ever stop this foolishness? Could it actually be from Josh?"

When Bob and FBI Agent Calio arrived, Mary was sitting at the kitchen table and crying and holding the crumpled letter in her hand. She was more upset then he had ever seen her in the past when she received one of these letters. Bob put his arms around her and told her, "Calm down sweetheart give me the letter. I'm sure we can handle whatever it says." Mary was weeping harder as she handed him the letter, "Bob, he said that he is going to kill you and a lot of others. I'm scared to death for us. Why did I ever agree to marry you? I have put you in a terrible position."

"Calm down Mary, I'm not afraid I face threats like that all the time in my job. It's just talk let me have the letter."

Mary handed Bob the letter. There was still no name or address was on the letter. It read "I love you. After all my warnings to you about marrying the policeman you went and did it anyway. I will not hold that against you. I have had a few women while I was away from you. I understand the sex drive. But I must put an end to this quandary now. Didn't I send you a nice diamond ring? I realize now that I can never become your husband as long as that wife stealer is alive. I tried my best to warn you. Evidently you did not believe me. You failed to heed my warning even after I got rid of Patrick O'Malley who was reported ready to marry you. I didn't know he was queer at the time and now that I know that to be true he would probably never marry a woman anyway. I acted in haste."

"But, my deal for you is this - you come live with me and I will make you the happiest women in a new town with a new ID and of course the children could come too I will be a good father to them. I discovered in the Midland paper that you were married to the cop.

You broke my heart, but I can and will take care of that problem. He will be a dead man soon."

"I have been doing everything that I could to let you know I love you. Why didn't you understand what I was doing? I think I am crazy trying to get you but I am now determined to have you. Naturally, I am not about to let that cop friend of yours know what my name is or where I am living so he can track me down. If you do as I say later, I will take you and the children away. If you will join me, we can share our lives together again with both children, I promise you that I will make you happier than you have ever been in your life. I have found the exact location where we can put everything together if you are willing to have me."

"I promise you the cop will not stand in my way. I plan on killing Bob Mitchell in the very near future. Why did you marry that damn cop after I asked you not to? I had made plans of just how we could have gotten together. You have made that impossible now. I will have to come up with a new plan. If I can't have you no one else ever will. I promise you that. Mark the following down so you can give it to your cop husband and tell him that I mean business. I can out fox him and I will put him to death."

"First I will kill that Jew boy Ed Stein. He came between us years ago. He told me that you were going to marry him and he told me to stay away from you. He may be dead by the time you get this letter. Second I will kill that cop husband of yours. He has taken advantage of your situation. Then it will be up to you, you can go off and live with me or I will kill us both. If I can't have you no one else will and my life would not be worth living."

"I will make you the happiest woman on earth at a distant place and see that you have everything one could possibly want like the ring I sent you. You will be looked upon as a queen. The choice is yours Mary Louise."

Bob read the letter over twice and asked Mary if she would let him have the letter for their files. Bob and the FBI agent began to leave and Bob told Mary "Don't worry sweetheart. I'll be home about six, OK?"

"Ok Bob, I have to go to the library to work until 5:00 tonight. Do lock the door on your way out."

That evening, Bob asked Mary to take the two children to stay with his parents in Boise, Idaho. The suspect would not know who her parents were or where they lived. He had talked to her mother and she would be more than happy to have them stay there. He assured her that their suspect would be found and in custody before school started in the fall. The kids would love the mountains and the open lands. Mary agreed but failed to convince Bob that he should join them in Idaho.

He told her, "I'm a policeman. I know how to take care of myself."

Mary left the next morning with the children and arrived safely in Boise in time for dinner.

Two days later, Josh stopped at his mail box to get

his mail. Since Mary and the children had gone to Boise, he had been staying at a motel as his Chief and the FBI had instructed him to do. He drove to his motel turned on his television to learn that President Obama had accepted General McChrytstal's resignation from the Afghanistan Command. Bob had been so busy he just had not been following the news. He began to open or discard the mail. He had in his hand, a letter addressed to his wife Mary. He opened the letter so he could read it to his wife when he called her after dinner.

The letter was postmarked in Pittsburgh, Pennsylvania. The letter contained only a few lines. Two down Mary - Number three on the way. You will be without that wife stealing husband soon. I love you and I need you. I will find a way to contact you after I take care of my business.

Bob did not tell Mary about this letter when he called. All he told her was that the FBI and his office were on top of the situation and they had already made contact with the air base in Universal City, Texas and the personnel office there were trying to establish a list of recruits that had been transferred to the Base in Dover.

If that was successful they felt that the number of air force employees would be greatly reduced. They were also working with the various civilian contractors to determine if they had made any transfers to Dover. Bob told her before he hung up, "Don't repeat this information to anyone, not even my parents. I love you and I miss you. I will try to join you in Boise for a few days the week after next."

The next day from the stakeout at Bob's house reported that an incoming call went to the answering service, but no message was recorded. Within a few minutes the call was found to have originated in Pittsburgh, Pennsylvania. Later that same day the stakeout at the library had an incoming long distant call come in and it had originated in Emory, Ohio.

The caller asked if Mary Mitchell was there, and as she had been instructed by the FBI the librarian told the caller that Mary was not working this week and that she was on vacation with her family. She would be back Monday morning. If it was an emergency and they did not find her before Monday she would take a message and give it to her Monday.

The caller then asked if she knew where she was vacationing because they needed to get in contact with her due to a family emergency.

The librarian told him that she did not know where they went, but she thought that they might be the Rose Lake Camp Ground at Rose Lake. She knew that they went there quite often to go sailing, but she was not sure he would find them there. She had been instructed to tell them that message should she be asked where Mary could be found. The librarian had done her job well. She had repeated Mary was out until Monday three times. The FBI sent two agents to the camp ground to watch for anyone entering the Park. All persons entering the Park had to have a pass to get by the gate, so it should be easy to watch at that point. The Park Manager was alerted that they were looking for a felon and the Manager agreed to help them.

He said the vast majority of his campers were from the Midland area and for the most part were well known by the gate employees. After Sunday afternoon they added additional agents to the stakeout. The two calls from Pennsylvania indicated that he was travelling west at that time. He could very well be in Michigan by now.

The FBI team in Universal City reported to their Headquarters that they had created a list of all personnel and airmen that had been officially transferred to or volunteered to go to Dover, Delaware the list was short. One civilian employee had asked for a transfer to Dover so he could be close to his family who lived in Cape May, NJ his name was Charles Wainwright a white male 26 years old.

He had been a mechanic and had just ended a tour in Afghanistan with the company a month ago. He had been in Afghanistan for two years. All others on the list were military.

There had been a total of twenty seven airmen who had been sent to Dover all were males except two who were female. The list contained their names, serial number, rank and date transferred. The list was in date transferred order. The first on the list to go to Dover was dated six years ago and the last entry was dated in January of the current year.

A message was typed on the list that a few of these transfers may have been for a short period of time with a temporary transfer and that the low number to this base was due to the operations performed at that base. Information on their personnel records after transfer to Dover would have to be obtained from the personnel office at the Dover base.

One of the names on that list was Joseph B Miller he had been transferred to Dover at his request to be closer to his family it was dated two years and four months ago. The FBI had a short list prepared to checkout and a team from the Philadelphia FBI office was on their way to Dover within hours after Texas had compiled the list. Midland police sent two detectives; Bob was not among them because they feared that the suspect may recognize him as they had met in earlier years. Jack Short and another officer from the Wilmington Police Department were also sent to Dover. They all met at the Air Base the next day.

The short list was broken down into three lists of nine names and the start of the questioning of these individuals began after eight of the names had been set aside because their transfer was made prior to reported death of Joshua Merritt, were female, or had been transferred to other bases or retired from the service before the date of the murder in Wilmington.

There were now nineteen names on the list and with

the cooperation of the Base Staff, a list of scheduled times was set up for each of the nineteen potential suspects. The FBI Team leader composed a set of thirty questions that were to be asked of each suspect.

Sixteen of the questions were routine questions. What is your name, your date of birth, your place of birth, your marriage status, any children, and other basic items such as military ID.

There were several questions that were to be asked solely to give the suspect the impression that he had been recommended for a special highly sensitive project that would involve a reassignment outside of the United States for approximately six months and that he would be required to be trained to speak a little of the Chinese language.

He would only need to learn a few basic words of the language that may be required to be understood during the operation should the need arise, such as the words: Food, Water, How far, Friend, etc. Did he think he could learn a few words of the language? Had he ever had any foreign language training? Did he have any problem with being out of contact with friends and relatives for a period up to six months?

The other questions were all case related and the suspect was told that they had been instructed to do a background check on each candidate and the project required that the candidate must not be aware of any of the people that would be a part of the project because these people would be involved with the project as civilians rather than military. Did he know any of the women in this picture and he was to be shown three pictures of three different women, all were white with similar features one of which was Mary Mitchell? Suspects reactions were to be noted especially when Mary's picture was shown. Had he ever been in any of the following states; asked one at a time, North Dakota, South Dakota, Iowa, Michigan, Maryland, DC, or Florida? All yes answers were to be asked what cities or towns and when he was there and doing what when there. The first seven men to be questioned were temporarily eliminated as a possible suspect, for one reason or another.

The eighth on the list was on leave and would be at the base in three days, he would be questioned on his return.

The ninth and tenth men on the list were on a flight to Afghanistan. They too would be questioned on their return for they had just left on the flight that day before.

The eleventh on the list was Joseph B Miller who was reported AWOL. He had been granted leave for two days and had failed to return to the base as scheduled the prior Friday. Friday was the date that Edward Stein had been murdered.

His military photo ID was immediately faxed to the FBI team in Midland Michigan. Bob faxed the photo to the Police Station in Boise, Idaho and asked them to pick up Mary and have her identify the picture and requested that they place a watch on his parent's home there because the photo may have identified a murderer and that the suspect had promised harm to Mary as well.

He was certain that the suspect was unaware of her location in Boise, but he was a pretty smart guy and may have found out.

Mary was taken to the station where she was shown the photo to Mary and she almost fainted.

"That's a picture of my dead husband Josh. His hair is cut shorter but that is him. See the little scar to the left of his nose?"

"He had a fish hook lodged there once when he was teaching my son to cast his line at the Lake and my Billy was just too young to do it right. A lure lodged in Josh's face when he attempted to make a cast. It had to be cut out at the ER and two stitches were required to close the cut. Yes, that is Josh."

"He must not have been in that car in the bad accident years ago?" Bob was contacted on the telephone and they told him exactly what Mary had told them. They then put her on the phone with Bob. "Yes, Bob that sure looks like a picture of Josh. Where is he? "Is he in the Army? I want to go home Bob, please let us come home."

"No, Mary, we do not know where he is at the moment or proof that he is indeed Josh. It is important that you stay where you are. It won't be long now.

"We know who we are looking for now and we will

have him soon. We are setting up traps for him. He will take our bait soon. He is in the Air Force and stationed at the Air base in Dover, Delaware. He is now AWOL and is also a suspect in Ed's death as well as the killer of Patrick O'Malley that he has admitted doing in a letter to you. Just give us a little more time. I love you and miss you and the kids terribly. Tell them I love them. I will call you again tonight. I will give more information at that time. I have to go Mary, I love you. Don't worry we have everything under control. Good bye darling."

Bob went back to the station and a plan was made in the hopes of catching the suspect. After the meeting he went to his motel to shower and then went to a restaurant nearby to have dinner. He would call her back after he had dinner.

Chapter Five

A search of AWOL Joe Miller's quarters on the Dover Air Base found proof that he had been in Paris because his credit card bill found in his dresser drawer revealed a large charge of over $5,000 for jewelry purchased from a jewelry store near the Eiffel Tower. Jack Short of the Wilmington police made a trip to Dover and checked with all the Auto Rental Firms in an attempt to determine if Joe Miller had rented a white Van as described by the witness thought to be a KIA.

The record was found at the Avis Agency in Dover. They stated that Joseph B Miller had rented a white Toyota on the Friday morning of Ed Stein's death and that the van had been returned to an Avis lot in Toledo, Ohio exactly as he was to do in the rental agreement. He had used cash to pay the fees. The girl on the counter told Jack, that he often rented vehicles from them.

Jack asked if they could determine if and when he

had rented a vehicle. She said that was possible and soon gave him a printout of his past rentals. Jack noted that there were several on the list but they failed to show destinations as the vehicles all were returned back to the Dover lot. He forwarded that list by fax to Bob in Midland, Michigan.

Bob checked the dates attempting to determine if they were near any of the mailing date on the parcels and letters that Mary had received. They were found to be within five days time of the items.

In Toledo it was determined that the van had been returned and the final bill was paid by cash. They were unable to help the FBI agent with any information that they did not already have. The van itself was no longer in Toledo it had been cleaned and rented several times.

Midland Police received a call from the FBI office in Chicago that the rental car had been dropped off in Toledo, Ohio. They had no further information but that it was assumed the suspect was on his way to Michigan to prepare for his second threat. They were wondering why he dropped off his rental car in Toledo. Was he trying to throw them off track? If he was on his way to Michigan how was he getting there? Perhaps he was planning a change of autos?

They suggested that other rental lots be scrutinized and that they attempt to determine if he had stayed at a motel, but they failed in doing that. There were far too many motels, and most of the ones that were checked did not have any records at all. They stopped that search because they were sure that he would not have rented the room in his own name and would have used cash instead of using his credit cars as he had done in his first rental.

Bob stopped by his house to get the mail. He did not open any of the mail as he was to attend an operation meeting with the FBI team. The meeting was just getting underway when he arrived at the station. Bob tossed the mail on his desk and joined the task force.

Jack Short from the Wilmington, Delaware Police Force had arrived in Midland earlier that day after learning that the suspect may be heading for Michigan. Bob had met Jack as usual at the airport. Jack briefed all in attendance on the murder of Edward Stein including the witness's statement that led them to Joe Miller.

Bob reported briefs on all of the letters and parcels that had been received and on his theory, which was now almost certain to be fact. The FBI agent in charge at this time, Fred Hopkins, reported that it was almost conclusive that the suspect was indeed Josh Merrill and that he had assumed the name of Joseph Barr Miller.

When they got deep into the background of Airman Miller, the records indicated that he was, living in Denton, Texas at the time he enlisted into the air force and the application forms were very accurate. He had accomplished a remarkable job in making his new ID look proper, but when a check was made on his social security number the record showed that the real Joseph

Miller had died and his widow was receiving his Social Security benefits.

It also showed that payments were still being added to the account and were being paid by the U S Air Force through the Defense Department. An adjustment of benefits would be necessary due to the additional funds being deposited in the account in error. The case had been assigned to the fraud unit for investigation because a death benefit had been paid. He stated that without any doubt someone had assumed the ID of the deceased Joseph Miller.

He made a point that when the photo of Josh held by the FBI and the photo of the real Joseph Miller was compared, Josh had done a good job in getting a fairly close resemblance. The only readily apparent difference was that Josh had a half inch visible scar on his right cheek. This scar should be added to all of their notes for identification.

Bob injected, "That is correct, Mary noted that difference when she was first shown the photo on Miller's military records."

The mystery now was, if this was indeed Josh Merrill, who was reported killed and burned in the auto crash, who was the person that actually was burned to death in that accident.

Bob told the team, "The Midland newspaper had received a letter from a lady in Ohio who was inquiring about her missing husband and that it had been over two years without any trace. She asked the paper if they could possibly run an article about her husband in hopes that someone may have some information as to his whereabouts."

"The paper decided to run a story on all of our unresolved cases to make it a broader feature story and I pulled our files out to determine if we had any missing persons outstanding and BINGO, I think I have our answer. We found a witness to the missing man and he may have been with Josh when last seen. The full story is in the report."

Agent Hopkins then went over their plans on how they might trap him if he did indeed plan to kill Bob as he had promised Mary that he would do.

Several nights later, a light was on in the living room of Bob's house and his image was as a shadow through the thin lace curtain over the window. Across the street from Bob's house was a panel truck that was from a Heating and Air Conditioning Repair Service with a Midland address. It had been parked there since 5:30 that evening. Inside the truck were two agents that were watching Bob's house for any activity.

One of the agents had just poured each of them a cup of coffee and they were each having a sandwich when they heard a loud gun shot. They pushed a button that automatically sent a message to headquarters that they were out of the car in pursuit of a suspect. After spilling their coffee in their laps as they rushed out of the van, they got a glimpse of someone dressed entirely in black running behind the shrubbery in Bob's backyard and through the yard of his back yard neighbor's house.

He jumped in a car parked on the street in back of Bob's house and sped off. Within a few minutes three patrol cars were at the scene and two of them sped off around the block to the back street and headed in the direction that the car was seen leaving the crime scene.

From the position where they were they were not in a position to shoot or identify the car, except they did know that it was a silver sedan. They got on their radio and put out an alert for a silver automobile car driving West on the 1600 block of Pine street. Little did they know that their suspect had pulled into a garage and closed the door behind him in the 1900 block of the same street when three patrol cars sped by.

A check of Bob's house revealed that a single shot had been fired though the window of the living room and had knocked the dummy that had been placed there out of its chair. The trap had succeeded in drawing the suspect to a specific location but they had made the mistake of not watching the street in back of Bob's house.

Back at the station, Bob got the report of the incident and was nervously playing with papers on his desk when he noticed the mail he had placed earlier on his desk. It was addressed to him and had been mailed locally in Midland. Mail collected in Midland addressed for local delivery is postmarked locally.

He opened the letter. It contained a single sheet of paper, with the inscription. "OK, So Mary is not home. You have her off somewhere where you think she is safe; I will find her sooner or later. BUT I want you first."

"I will find you in my gun sight when you least expect me. Are you having fun waiting for me to find you? I have all the time I need to catch you off guard. Keep looking over your shoulder I may be in back of you. You can't hide in the Police station all the time. I'll get you soon -- you wife stealer." It was not signed.

Bob checked the date of mailing it had been sent just the previous day before this attempt to kill him was made. He told the task force that he wished he had picked up his mail earlier because they would have known that he was in the area and the trap would have worked because they would have expanded the watch to a larger perimeter of the area, including the back street. The next morning, the local newspaper's front page contained a headline in Bold large type that read,"BACK FROM THE DEAD" and went on to read "Local man, Josh Merrill, thought to have been killed over three years ago in a fiery accident, appears in Midland again and makes an attempt to kill his wife's new husband." The article went on to print the details of the attempt and mentioned that he had eluded capture driving away in a silver or grey sedan."

Josh picked up a newspaper at an area convenience store paper dispenser and returned to his rented house where he read the entire story. He was shocked to read he had missed his target. He could not believe that Bob was still alive, he saw the body fall from the chair.

He assumed that they probably suspected that he was still in Midland and was thought to be driving a silver car. He decided to abandon the car and leave it in the garage of his rented house out of view. He had to get away from Midland very quick. Everyone including Mary and Bob now knew that he was alive. He was now on a criminal wanted list for sure. He had to disappear again and get another ID. He knew that he could not go back to the Dover airbase. Joe Miller was AWOL and was now a suspect in the death of Ed Stein. And probably they knew by his stupid letter that he had also killed Patrick O'Malley.

He had rented the completely furnished house the day he arrived in Midland. He had paid the first month's rent in cash and he also used cash to pay the security deposit. He told his landlord, a woman in her 40's, he was in the area looking for a home to buy.

He said he needed a much larger house then her rental. His wife and family were in Boise, Idaho and she would be arriving as soon as he had some possible homes lied up to view and make a purchase. He was going to open up an electrical construction business in Midland. He had told her that with the housing market being as it was, more people were remodeling their older homes and licensed electricians and handymen were needed everywhere.

The rental home was located just a few blocks

from Bob's house and was situated on the street in back of Bob's home. He thought how convenient it would be to hide in quickly after he did his kill. But he was aware that it was not a place for him to be at this time. He locked the door and walked back toward the convenience store and hailed a cab, while carrying a grocery bag in his arms. He directed the cab driver to take him to an auto repair shop on the corner of Myrtle Street and Eighth Avenue. He had made note of that shop when he was checking out a route to leave Midland in a hurry. He told the cab driver that his car was in the repair shop and he needed to get to Detroit for a meeting the next day.

"I'm representing our union and we want to know just what is going to happen to our Union pension funds should the parts plant where they worked was to shut down. Damn politicians have everything fouled up."

The cab driver agreed with Josh's statements and added just as they arrived at the repair shop, "They sure have, I'm going to vote against every one of them if they are running for reelection. I'm hoping that new tea party group can get us some honest people to run who have our interests at heart instead of their own wallets as it is now."

Josh agreed, "Yes me too. Thanks – What's your name, I'll ask for you when I get back from Detroit the day after tomorrow?"

"Just ask for Rick, I'm the only driver named Rick." Josh gave him a $5.00 tip.

"Thanks."

About fifteen minutes after Josh had left the house a call was received at the police station. The lady who owned the house which was situated next door to her own home was calling to tell them that she was sure that her new tenant was Josh Merrill.

When she rented the house to him earlier that week she had told her husband how much he looked like Josh Merrill who used to go to her church that was killed in an accident a few years back. She read in the paper this morning the story about Josh being alive and his attempt to murder the policeman that had married his wife. She told the clerk on the phone, "You know her Barbara she's the girl who works in the library on the front desk."

She was very excited and finally Barbara, the clerk on the police desk interrupted her by telling her, "Yes, we know all that but I'm going let you talk to one of our officers.

"I am calling to tell you that I think and I am rather certain, that I rented one of my houses to that Joshua Merrill earlier this week. He just left the house walking down the street. I don't know why he didn't take his car."

The desk clerk rang Bob's phone on his desk and told him to get on line one quick. Bob took the call and the lady calling repeated everything that had already been told to the desk clerk. He asked the lady calling what her name was and the address of the house that she had rented. Was she sure that he left walking? In what direction was he walking and thanked the lady, telling her that a police officer would be talking to her in a few minutes. He hung up after thanking her.

Three cars were sent to the street on which he was reported to be walking.

The cab driver had picked up Josh as he hailed his cab. They were heading in the opposite direction, when two police cars approached the cab with sirens blasting away. The cab driver told Josh, "Boy, there must be a bad accident up the road somewhere; they sure e are in a hurry."

Josh lied and said, "Yes, I think it must be a bad fire. Two fire trucks went flying back there a few minutes before you picked me up." Josh knew that he was within walking distance to the Hertz rental lot. He had told the cab driver when he picked him up to drop him off at that auto garage on Myrtle Street and Eighth Avenue, "I hope they have my car finished."

He paid the cabbie and when the cab was out of sight crossed the street walked to the Hertz lot. He discarded his grocery bag that was full of old newspapers in a dumpster on the corner of the rental lot. He wondered how long it would take for the landlord to know that he had vacated her house and had left his rented silver car in the garage.

Josh used cash to rent another vehicle. He chose a maroon two door Chevy. He left immediately and drove east away from Midland. He realized that he was running out of cash, and that it would only be a short time before the police got to his credit card to start tracking him. He decided he had to quit using the card because they could track where he was at the time he used it. He had to start using cash. He still had the gun which he used in his attempt to kill the policeman and decided he had nothing to lose he must find some cash. And the gun should help him.

He left the highway and drove to a small town and went to a prosperous looking liquor store and parked out of sight in a public parking lot. He entered the store ordered a bottle of whiskey and then pulled his gun from his jacket pocket when the clerk was away from the counter.

He then ordered the clerk to keep his hands in the air and come to the counter and open the cash drawer. The clerk did as he was told. Josh pocketed the cash and pulled the trigger of his gun. "What the hell, that was easy." He was soon on the road again and this time had a pocket full of cash.

He decided that he must find a place to think over his situation. "Damn, how did I miss that son of a bitch? I know I hit him. I saw him fall out of the chair when I shot." The newspaper didn't say anything about Bob. "Maybe I did kill him and they don't want me to think I did, yes that's it. No, the paper said I made an attempt – that means I didn't kill him." "I know I hit him. He didn't die, but was hit, that's it. How can I find out if he's hurt? Will he live? Where is he is now? How bad was he hurt?"

He decided he had better just lay low, and get far away. He can wait to find out. He drove through the night and found a motel in Pennsylvania. Just off the turnpike. The car rentals were keeping him strapped for cash and would eventually be traced to him. He decided that he needed to find a place where there was public transportation. He decided that he would stop in Harrisburg and stay there until things quieted down, and until he could find out Josh's condition.

He would call the police station in Midland, from a phone booth of course, and ask for Bob. Just maybe they may give him the answer. He would get back on the Pennsylvania turnpike in the morning and make the call from there.

He found a bar in the capitol city and had a few beers and made conversation with a prostitute. He spent $50.00 of his liquor store robbery on the prostitute in his room and after he had left his rented vehicle in a theater parking area near his motel. He decided that he would just lay low for awhile right there in Harrisburg or in the area. He would deliver the car to Hertz in the morning so that it would not be reported as stolen to the police. Perhaps he could find a job to stay in funds.

Bob was very upset with everyone, especially the desk clerk, who took the call from the landlord, "Had we been just a few minutes earlier we would have had that bastard." The desk clerk told Bob he had a call on line two. He picked up the phone and there was no one on the line.

He asked the desk clerk if she got any information on the call and she said that she had. She told Bob, "The caller told me he wants to talk to you only, it was not police business, something about a dog you had for sale. I didn't know you had a dog."

"I don't". Bob picked up the phone and the caller had hung up. "Now the SOB knows that I am alive and not wounded. Tell Fred to call off the hospital surveillance."

Across the street from his cheap motel in a rundown area of Elizabethtown, Pennsylvania was a truck repair shop. Josh noticed a "Help Wanted" sign in the window. He walked over to the shop and inquired about the job. He told the manager that he had just been discharged from the air force and that he was a mechanic and worked on plane engines, as well as the trucks and cars on the base.

He was hired in a matter of minutes and was put to work following the interview. There was a backup of trucks needing service. He used his air force ID for identification when asked. Joseph B Miller was now a mechanic with a job. The shop had agreed to loan him a set of tools, but that he would have to get his own tools to stay on the job. It was a happy day for him. He was tired of hiding and he loved working as a mechanic.

Earlier he had read about persons using stolen social security numbers for tax purposes and to get merchandise or jobs who were apprehended when they used a card that had been stolen. He didn't think about that when he was in the military. He couldn't figure out how that was done, but that was history now.

When applying for this new job he read off the SS# to the girl in the office and quoted her a new number that had three different numbers in it. He would have her change it later to a new number after he got a new ID. He would tell her she had not sent the right number when she sent his payroll deduction to the IRS. He had time to get that all straightened out after he got the ID. But every time he had a little too much to drink, which was most of the time now, the urge to kill Bob kept him awake at nights. He gave little thought to Mary and the children. He was certain that he would never get Mary back now.

He was obsessed more than ever to kill Bob. He had convinced himself that he would have been able to get Mary to join him had it not been for Bob. The little children, one of which was his own, had no part in his troubles and he really had no reason to kill them or Mary. He was happy that he had killed Billy's dad. He just had to settle the matter with Bob. He would find a way.

He was obsessed more than ever now and had worked himself up to the point to do it when he went on vacation in a few months. But he needed a plan that would not fail.

After receiving three paychecks, he had been able to

buy a used automobile. He signed the sales agreement in the name of Joe W. Selby whose identity he had assumed using the same method that he had attained the identity of Joe Miller. He gave his address in Harrisburg as his residence.

He had rented an apartment with a Harrisburg address just off of Interstate 81. He had let his hair grow and it was almost to his shoulders and had let the hair on his face grow. It was all neatly trimmed by a barber. He looked in the mirror and decided that he had a neat appearance and felt that he could go anywhere now without fear of being noticed.

Even the scar on his cheek was now hidden under the short growth of facial hair. He had bought a pair of glasses to use when he began his pursuit of Bob. He decided that he would no longer send those letters to keep them frightened all the time. He would wait until they let down their guards. But he really did enjoy keeping them in fear, he might reconsider writing again.

He searched the newspapers and soon found another trucking firm that was looking for an experienced mechanic. He applied for the position and Joseph W Selby was now a mechanic for a very large trucking company located in Elizabethtown, .Pennsylvania that locals referred to as E'town.

He had looked for and had found a new ID with the first name of Joseph. He was used to having people call him with that name and he would be able to use that same first name. After obtaining his new ID he left the trucking company where he had been employed as J Barr Miller. Joe Barr Miller was no longer used. He was now Joe W. Selby. It had been six months since his last trip to Michigan where he had attempted to kill Bob, and he did kill the guy in the liquor store out there somewhere. He couldn't remember the name of that little town. He had not made any contact with the Mitchell's since that terrible night. Things should be getting back to normal now, he thought. It should be easy this time but he had to have a plan. The one thing that he was going to do was to stop writing to Mary or Bob. How stupid I was in letting them know of my every plan.

Mary had returned to Midland and was entering the hospital to give birth to Bob's first child. The doctor had told Mary and Bob it would be a boy. Bob's mother was in Midland and was waiting for the big event. She had accepted Mary's children just as if they had been Bob's children, but the thought of her being a blood grandmother had her excited. She would not let Mary do anything but rest.

She was doing the cooking, the laundry, and the housekeeping. Mary was actually embarrassed about the way her mother-in-law was watching over her. Their new home was still on a routine check three times a day but there was no surveillance. They had moved to this new home just a month ago to have an extra bedroom that they would need after the birth of their new son.

Billy and Nancy would be approaching the age in the next future where they could not share a room together. Until then, the extra room in the new house could be used by the grandparents on their annual trips to visit with Bob and Mary.

A fellow worker in the same garage repair shop as Josh, named Wayne, had become a close friend of Josh and they bowled in a league together often. Wayne had told Bob that his wife had been appointed a census taker.

One Saturday afternoon Josh stopped at Wayne's house to watch a football game with him. Josh told Wayne's wife Ellen, that Wayne had told him that she was going to be a census taker and that her job was to interview the residents of a house who had failed to mail in their census forms.

She said, "Yes, here's my ID Joe – isn't my photo just terrible?" and she handed him the ID to see for himself, while she went to the kitchen to get them both another beer. Josh looked at the picture and replied,"Looks pretty good to me, I bet you're the prettiest girl in E'Town who will be taking the census. All you have to do is ask questions on the form like the one that was mailed to them. Is that it?"

Ellen returned from the kitchen and handed the tray with some potato chips and a spread of some sort on it that she was carrying. She said "That's it Joe. The only thing that I won't like is working in some of the areas that I will be assigned to. Some are pretty seedy neighborhoods and some of the people in those areas are really pretty frightening to be around."

She bent over Josh to make way for the tray on the coffee table and facing Josh. Josh noticed that she was not wearing a bra and her breasts were well exposed. She caught Josh's eyes looking at her breasts, winked at him and smiled. Josh smiled back.

Josh slipped the ID he was holding in his shirt pocket when she handed him the tray to place on the coffee table as she moved some items on the table to make way for the tray. The conversation quickly changed. After watching the Florida Gators play a football game with Florida State, Josh said he had to go. The Florida Gators had won the game, and Josh was pleased with that. He had always been a fan of Michigan State, but he had always been a fan of the Gators that was started when he was in Florida over the winter weeks that he was in Florida. That felt like it was a long time ago.

When he got home, he found the Census ID that had been left in his shirt. He called Wayne, and told him that he had the ID and how it got in his pocket. He had forgotten that he had it in his shirt pocket. He asked if Ellen would need it before Monday and Wayne told Josh, No.

Josh said, "Well in that case, I'll drop it off to you tomorrow when I leave the Library. The Library doesn't open until noon, so it will be about three when I leave. Will that be OK and will you be home?"

Wayne said they would be home and that would

be OK. "What will you be doing at the library; I don't know how you find the time to read?"

"I don't read much, but I go there to copy things I want to make a few copies of some items I want to keep. He actually had a few newspaper articles that were written after his attempt to kill Bob." As Josh was copying his papers he got an idea that perhaps this may be a way to gain access to Bob's house without detection. He could pose as a census taker and walk right up and down the street surrounding Bob and Mary's house and even go to their front door without detection.

He could even move his car from house to house and he would see if there was any surveillance being done when he was in the area. He was sure that the Census ID could be valuable to him even if he found a better plan later. All he would have to do was replace the photograph with one of his own and redo the typed data on the Census ID form.

He would give that some thought and he made several color copies of Ellen's ID. After leaving the library he stopped by Wayne's house to leave Ellen's ID as he had promised. There were a few minutes before Ellen answered the door. She had hollered asking who it was, and Josh replied, "It's me, Josh, I have your ID."

Ellen asked him to wait just a minute. Her hair was still wet from the shower when she opened the door for Josh and invited him in. She was dressed only in a robe, and told Josh, "Joe, you caught me just as I was getting out of the shower. Wayne got a call this morning and was asked to go to see the Steelers game and the guy that called him said he had an extra ticket. Wayne jumped at the chance to see a home game. He will not be home until after the game around five this afternoon. Would you like a cold beer?"

Josh told her,"That sounds good, sure." He gave her the ID and told her that he was sorry that he had taken the card without knowing that he had done so until he got home. Ellen replied, "No problem Joe, I am happy that you did. I thought that you did it deliberately. I knew you had it all the time. I was hoping that you would deliver it to me sometime when Wayne was away. Here we are and he is away."

Josh had become attracted to Ellen over the past several months, and on several occasions she had made several similar passes at him. Josh had always ignored them, but as they were now alone and Ellen was sitting on the sofa as close as she could be with her legs exposed high on her thighs, Josh could no longer pass up such an opportunity.

"I appreciate the opportunity of being alone with you. You are everything I like in a man and have all of the things that Wayne does not have. Wayne told me that you were divorced and were using whores. I'm not a whore Joe, but can't you pretend that I am? Of course I will not charge you." She stood up and dropped her robe to the floor. She was totally nude. Josh, stood up, took her in his arms and whispered in her ear as he fondled her breasts, "I have been hoping for a moment like this every since Wayne introduced me to you."

They went into the bedroom together. Later Ellen asked Josh when they could get together again.

Josh told her, "Soon, I hope, because I will be on vacation in a few weeks and I will be away for about a week to ten days. I will want you again before then for sure. I don't want Wayne to know anything about this afternoon Ellen so we have to be careful, mighty careful." They kissed and Josh left.

Josh had been home for about 30 minutes and received a phone call. It was Ellen. "Joe, I just thought of something. I will make up a story to tell Wayne that I would like to visit one of my High school friends that I hadn't seen in years and that I had a call from her inviting me to Chicago so we could see some shows and go visit a few of our school friends who live in Illinois. I will tell him that the girls would join me for a week so we all could attend our high school reunion. I am certain that Wayne will agree especially now that the deer season is about to open here in Pennsylvania. He always takes a week off then to go with a gang of his friends to a hunting camp up in Union county. I could accompany you on your trip to Michigan. What do you think about that?"

Josh told her, "Ellen, I would love to have you with me as I go to Michigan, but on this trip I will be preoccupied with some business there that I must take care of. I have been trying to close my divorce case with my Ex for over three years. And I think that the time has come for me to finalize that transaction."

"I hope you can understand, but I will be finalizing a divorce settlement and I can't be seen with a woman before the case is closed as it may once again postpone the settlement that my attorney has suggested to my Ex and her attorney said she is prepared to accept it."

"Her case has me proven as an adulterer and I have been squeaky clean in that area when I am around our mutual friends. I can't risk any question in the eyes of the judge or her attorney. "

"Her attorney is a pain in the butt; he tries to watch my every move to strengthen her case. He doesn't know it, but I was messing with his own secretary. She's a pretty gal and loves sex but she is not half the woman you are. She calls me when he or one of his sleuths is coming to check on me."

"Now, you know why I can't take you to Michigan? It is a case of dollars and cents. If they rule for my Ex it will cost me big time and if they cannot prove her allegations, I will save a lot of money. Do you understand?"

"Yes, I can see why now. I will wait for you and hopefully we can celebrate your winning the divorce settlement. That will be worth the wait. If things go well between the two of us, I will get rid of Wayne. Then we could be together all the time."

Josh, smiled he had made up that divorce thing and Ellen had bought it. He wanted nothing to get in his way of disposing of Bob this time. He had a plan. He asked, "Ellen has anyone started taking the census yet?"

"The census forms have been mailed, but the follow-ups, like my job, won't start until the third week of next month here in E'Town."

Josh continued to ask her about the type of questions she had to ask, If and when she had to show them her ID, What did she have to do if the person was not at home.

He had plans to use that Census ID to gain entrance to Bob's house and if there was surveillance in the area, he would be considered a census guy, just doing his job. All he needed was to get in the house. He would wait for Bob to come home.

This will work, he thought; he could come and go as he needed. He needed to test the silencer he had purchased. How much of a noise would it still make when the gun was fired. Would they be able to hear it, say 100 yards away? He had a lot of work to do. He found himself anxious to out fox those cops. Were they even still waiting for him to make his second attempt?

"Call me when you can meet me somewhere in the next few days. You are one great lover."

"She replied, "You are too. I have got to find a way to get Wayne away for a few hours some night. I want you. I don't love him anymore. I'll have to cook up some story to get a divorce." Josh tried to make up his mind. Should he take Ellen part of the way with him or should he go there alone. It had been a long time since he had spent a night with a woman who wasn't being paid to do so. After all she certainly was one good lover.

If Wayne was out of the picture he knew that she would marry him in a minute. But he could not forget his mission. Bob had to be killed. He no longer really needed Mary. Ellen would make a great mate. With Ellen there was a future he thought. Things could get back to normal in his life. Wayne had to be out of the picture.

Josh told Wayne and Ellen that he would be leaving after breakfast on Wednesday morning the day that his vacation was scheduled to begin knowing that he would not be leaving Pennsylvania until the weekend. He also told his landlady that he would be leaving on Wednesday and he rented a motel in Harrisburg for two nights so that it would appear that he had left E'Town on Wednesday as he was telling them.

On Friday evening he placed a call to Wayne and Ellen telling them that he was in Canton, Ohio and that he had had a nice trip. He told them he would be going to Michigan the next morning and asked Wayne if he would stop by his mail box and pick up his mail. He had forgotten to tell the post office to hold his mail. Wayne told him that he would do so. Josh was actually in a motel in Harrisburg, Pennsylvania.

Josh drove past Wayne and Ellen's house. It was two in the morning on Friday. The lights were all out. He walked quietly up the steps and unscrewed the bulb in the porch light fixture. He then took the handle of his gun and broke the glass out of the living room window.

He waited for Wayne to turn on the lights in the living room, and with the silencer on his pistol, shot Wayne two times. He then ran down the steps, and jumped in his car that was at the end of the driveway, with the motor running and disappeared in the dark.

When he arrived back at the motel, he fixed himself a drink and went to bed and left the next morning for his trip to Michigan. His absence from Elizabethtown on the night of Wayne's shooting and death had now been established.

Saturday evening after arriving in Toledo he called Ellen. She was hysterical. "Joe, someone broke into our house last night and they shot Wayne. They rushed him to the hospital but they could not save him he is dead?" Josh acted surprised "Did they get the person that shot him?""No, the police came after my neighbor called them. They are here at my house at this time. I can't talk to you now. She did tell Josh that her neighbor told them she had heard the shot, but was afraid to look out the window. She said a car went flying down the street but she did not see it.

"Who in the world would try braking into our house, we have nothing worth stealing?" Whispering she said, "I wanted to leave Wayne but not like this. Hopefully we can get together again after you get back from Michigan."

"My sister is coming to stay with me for a while. I'm afraid to stay here alone. The police caught a young boy who broke into a house down the street. But he said he didn't break into our house, and I don't think he did either. He didn't have a car when he was caught down the street. He was high on some type of drug."

Josh told her that he would stop over after he returned from Michigan to see her. He went to bed happy that Ellen would now be free and that all went as he had planned. He would have Ellen join him sometime after he came back from Michigan.

After several days, Josh called Ellen again and said that he would be leaving and that he would be back in about a week. They could have dinner together and discuss their future.

He had actually enjoyed killing Wayne. He was so proud of his action and how easy it was done he decided to send yet another letter to Bob and Mary. He wanted it to be more of a challenge when he actually got to Michigan. He wanted Bob to fear for his life. He was certain that he could out fox him and that would be fun in watching him sweating out his every move.

He wrote the letter and addressed it to Bob this time. It was a short note that read; "Hello Bob, I would bet that you had thought that I had given up on you. A lot has happened since I left Michigan some time ago, after I thought that I had killed you. Just last night I killed a man who was in the way of my future plans. Now the only thing that I need to do so I can accomplish my life's new goal is to see that your future plans will have ended. Three down now and you will make four."

Josh mailed the letter in the state of Indiana the next day. After mailing the letter, he began planning how he would get to Bob. As the day lingered on he began to wish he had not mailed that letter, because in doing so, he had lost all the advantage that the months of silence had given him. Why do I keep letting him know of my intentions? Josh was studying his plan. He knew that Bob was a policeman and he was sure to know how to protect himself. "I have to be smart. I am the cat and Bob is the mouse."

The next evening he stopped for the night on the outskirts of Midland. He made a call to Ellen. He asked her if the police had found out who shot Wayne. She said that they had not found anyone yet but they were working on it. She told him that she wished she was there with him.

She whispered to him, "I cannot say anymore because her sister was still at her house, I love you." Bob told her, "I love you too." He went to the bar across the street from his motel and looked for a prostitute. He found none. A gay approached him after Josh had inquired about a prostitute and Josh punched him in the face and then went to his room.

In Michigan he had removed his Pennsylvania license plates on his car and installed a set of Michigan tags that he had removed from a used car lot near his motel. He had to be more careful. The missing tags could be on the police lists before he needed them to hide his Pennsylvania tags, so he replaced the stolen Michigan tags with his own Pennsylvania tags. He placed the Michigan tags in his trunk. Good move he convinced himself. He had to remember to think as a cop would think.

He looked at himself in the mirror and convinced himself again that he would not be recognized as Josh Merrill. His beard and long hair had changed his appearance completely and with the glasses he absolutely had a different appearance from any one that ever knew him in Midland. Even Mary would not recognize him. He was getting himself worked up to challenge the authorities in Midland.

Little did Josh know that Bob had alerted the FBI that he had received a letter from Josh, and may be on his way back to Michigan or that the FBI team had already had their artist draw up pictures of Josh, with a crew cut, long hair and a beard, just a mustache, aged five years, and others possibilities, all of which were distributed to the entire police force. One of them was very close to his own present likeness.

He went to a clothing store and bought a white shirt and a tie. He brought a sports jacket with him. He was going to make himself into a census taker. He had his credentials which looked authentic, unless you looked very carefully and had an original to compare it with. Only then could his census ID be recognized as a fake. He had copied about fifty blank forms from the originals all in color, at the library in Elizabethtown. They were exact copies. All of this was in Ellen's black brief case that had been issued to her which Josh had stolen from her without her knowledge. She told her supervisor that she must have left it at one of her training classes. She was given a new one.

He checked everything out once again including his small revolver and silencer, which he had placed in the brief case under a flap that was intended to hold the completed census forms. He double checked that the revolver was loaded and that he had spare bullets.

He placed a call and made reservations at a hotel in mid city Midland. The hotel had an easy access to the expressway and was close to Mary's house. It was also only a short distance to the city building that housed the Police Department. That would be convenient for him to do his own surveillance. He used the name of Joseph Gibbons that he had placed on his Census ID and told them he would be taking a follow up census in the area and would need internet access.

They told him that the internet was available and that there was a restaurant and a lounge in the hotel itself. His restaurant charges and any bar items could be charged to his room. They were used to working with government employees and told him he would be billed weekly as they usually requested.

He took a shower and watched the news and soon went to bed. He was so excited that he was about to seek out his prey that he had a hard time getting to sleep.

In the morning he decided that he would not dress as a census taker until after he got checked into the hotel and started to initiate his plans. He put on casual clothes, had breakfast and left for Midland. He was surprised that the city had changed so much in the year since he was last there. There had been many changes in traffic patterns and a new bypass was now completed.

He recognized that he should travel around the areas where he was interested in going to. He had to learn all possible escape routes. He would start making a few runs through the areas as soon as he had checked in and had lunch. He had to stay focused on his mission. He would soon be matching wits with professionals.

He checked in telling the desk clerk that he had a reservation in the name of Joe Gibbons. They found the reservation and he was assigned a room on the ground floor as he had requested. He told the clerk "I have a fear of fires and always prefer the first floor so he could exit though the doors that opened directly to the outside." They had found one for him.

He went to his room and unpacked his one suitcase and went to lunch in the hotel restaurant. He remembered that he was to wear his glasses at all times now that he was in Midland. He was taken to a table that had been set up for two persons, and ordered his lunch.

At the table next to him, were four men, all neatly dressed and chatting about a show that they had been watching on TV the night before. Josh caught the eye of one of them and asked, "Are you here to take the census too?"

The man told Josh, "No, we are here to conduct a meeting for the local bank supervisors. Are you one of those census takers?"

"Yes, I have over a hundred people on my list that did not return the form that was mailed to them."

"Oh, I didn't think that they had started the follow up surveys yet. My sister is going to do the census follow up in Detroit and I thought she said that it would be about two or three weeks before they started."

Josh had to think fast, "Yes, that's true, but I am here to line up the routes the takers will be using when they do start."

Another man put his cell phone to his head, made a check of his cell phone and said, "OK, guys they are waiting for us at the bank. We have to go." After the four men left the restaurant, the one that had talked with Josh told his partners, "Did you notice how much he looked like one of the drawings we got this morning?"

Another said ,"Yes, I did notice that and I thought we need to put a tail on him. I got his picture on my cell phone."

When josh left the hotel parking area a maroon colored automobile across the street pulled into the traffic and followed Josh until he pulled into a street of residential homes. Josh parked his car. The car that was following him did not turn into the street. Josh did not see the car that was following him but he did see a white car that stopped on the other side of the street coming in from the other direction pull to a stop up the street in the opposite direction. Was he being followed he thought. Josh was shook up. The census takers were evidently not working yet. His plans were for naught. He better pull over to the curb and make a pretense that he was working with papers.

He drove to about four different streets and parked on each street and went thru a shuffling of his maps and some papers. He did not see the red car or the white car at any of his stops after the first one.

Josh decided that he was being overly cautious and decided to have lunch and give some thoughts as to what he could do now. Apparently the census plan was out of the question.

The agent in the white car reported to his team leader that the individual he was watching had made a total of seven stops during the morning and had stopped at the post office and had mailed an armful of envelopes. Josh had gone in the post office and placed his maps and papers in the lobby trash barrel.

The men tailing him did not come into the lobby. If there was indeed someone watching him he felt safer. He left the post office and drove to a small shopping area where he went in and out of a few shops there and left the mall to have lunch. He remembered that there was a restaurant across the street from the police station and decided to go there to see if he could see any activity there. If he was lucky he may see Bob leave and he could follow him where he could complete his task.

A picture was printed from the cell phone camera of Agent Wilkerson, and it was shown to Mary. Mary said "No, that's not Josh. I'm sure that is not Josh. Josh was a lot heavier then that guy.

The team compared the picture from the cell phone with the Military photo. They agreed that the individual in the new photo appeared smaller then the military photo. They called off the tail of Josh.

Chapter Six

Josh was a happy man. He had walked all over the area evidently without being recognized but his plan on getting in Mary's house as a census taker was now out of the question. They were not doing that yet. Maybe he could pose as a parcel delivery man. Yes he would look into that.

He would feel better if he had not sent that stupid letter warning Bob that he was on the prowl again. How stupid can I be he thought. I have just got to watch my every move and watch what I say. Mary and Bob both work and would not be at home during the day. He had to find a way for Bob to go to his home during the day.

He went to a restaurant that was situated across the street from the Police Headquarters. Perhaps he could see Bob going to or from the building and learn if Bob had a routine when he left work. He was sure that he would recognize him. He had a picture of Bob and Mary that was in the paper when they got married.

As he was sitting at his table with a cup of coffee, a newspaper, and a slice of pie, he saw four men get out of a car parked at the curb right outside his window. They looked familiar and he watched them cross the street and enter the police headquarters. Oh yes, those were the four that sat next to him at the hotel restaurant.

What were they doing going into Police Headquarters. I bet those SOB's lied to me, they are probably FBI agents. He became frightened. This was his first serious thought that he was indeed a murdering killer. He had already killed three men. He thought that he was being tailed this morning, but the car had turned off when he changed his direction onto Elm Street and he never saw it again. "But why am I worried about them. They don't know who I am, or they would have taken me this morning at breakfast." But he could take no chances. He quickly paid for his coffee and pie then got in his car and slowly drove onto the expressway and watched his mirrors for any cars tailing him. He saw none. He was glad that he had now placed the stolen Michigan tag on his car and that he had removed his Pennsylvania tag in the morning.

He drove to Bay City, and checked into a small motel at the edge of the town. He was glad that he had his brief case and his gun in the trunk of his car. He lost his suitcase and clothes. He was afraid to go back.

He had paid for a week so they would not be looking for him for not paying the bill.

After he was in his room at the new motel he decided to find a bar and have a few drinks, He needed to completely come up with a new plan. Maybe the parcel delivering guise would work. In the bar he was confronted by a pretty young girl of no more than 25 years of age. He recognized her for what she was, and told her "Not tonight honey, maybe tomorrow evening."

He left the bar and locked the doors to his room and placed a call to Ellen back in Pennsylvania.

Ellen answered the phone, "Hello Joe, I'm glad that you called."

"I miss you Ellen I sure wish you were here. What's new? Did they find out who shot Wayne yet?"

"No, not yet Joe, but that is why I said that I was glad you called. The detectives were here this morning asking me a thousand questions. I think they suspect that I had something to do with his death, and you know that I didn't. Don't you? They asked if I had been seeing another man. I lied."

"Yes, I am sure you didn't kill Wayne but you did say you wished you could get rid of him. You didn't kill him did you Ellen?"

"No. I did not. I hope you know better than that. To tell you the truth I was afraid that you may have done it especially after they questioned me about other men in my life and after the police kept asking questions about you. But I knew you were on your trip and couldn't have done it and I told them that."

Yes, I called you from Ohio if you remember. Oh, what did they say?" "Well, they knew you worked with Wayne and that we three were friends and had been seen together. They wanted to know where you were. I told them I did not know - out west somewhere, I thought. I told them that you were in Ohio on Wednesday when Wayne was murdered. You better hold your motel receipts in case you have to prove that. They told me that they had some questions they wanted to ask of you."

"Did they ask you what the questions were?"

"I asked them that and they said it had something to do with your military service. They didn't go any further than that."

Josh had no receipts and that could now be a problem. Perhaps he could get Ellen t o join him now and they could get a new ID and disappear. Ellen, I need you, can you possibly get away and meet me in Toledo as we had planned before all this happened?"

"Not now, Joe, the police told me not to leave town unless I cleared it with them. They said that whoever killed Wayne, may be looking for me too, but I don't think so because he broke the window to get in the house and we heard it in our bedroom, and Wayne ran in the front room to see what had happened. I think he was going to steal something, probably our new TV. That's about all we have with any value. I'm scared to death Joe. When will you be home? Is your divorce finalized yet?"

"No, the divorce is not completely finalized but it should be done before the end of the week. At least that is what my lawyer says." Josh suddenly thought that Ellen's phone may be tapped, so he lied, "I should be home by next Tuesday, I have to make a short trip up to Canada tomorrow morning, to get some papers signed, and I should be back in E'town by next Tuesday afternoon. There is a good chance that I may be awarded full custody of my daughter-- I have to go now Ellen, my lawyer is at the door. I love you. Bye."

Josh was glad that Ellen had mentioned about him calling her from Ohio. That may throw them off and let them think that I had nothing to do with killing Wayne. Josh left the motel as soon as he got off the phone in a fright and drove back to the bar and planned to stay there until almost midnight. He found a table that had a window where he could observe the motel parking area. If Ellen's phone had been tapped he was sure that someone would be checking the motel in a short time, and he was correct. In less than an hour, two police cars quietly pulled into the parking lot and two policemen got out of one car as the other one parked and blocked the exit out of the lot as the two knocked on the door. Josh quickly got in his car and drove to Flint, Michigan where he found a motel for the night. He checked his cash and realized that he had to get some additional cash soon. He did not like this running. He decided that he had to get this thing with Bob over with and quickly, but how?

The census plan was out of the question. He could not make up his mind as to whether the Pennsylvania police would know about his real name and the caper with Bob and Mary. He could not sleep, but he then remembered that Ellen had told him that the police wanted to talk to him about his military service. He was now AWOL and he knew he was now a federal case. I sure can't use my Joe Miller credit card anymore where I plan to stay for any time. They would surely be tracking where I used the card and that would keep them on my trail all the time. I'm probably near my limit anyway and I haven't made any payments for over a month now.

He was in need of cash and he knew how to take care of that situation. He undid his pony tail and let his long hair fall loose and then removed his baseball cap and jacket and drove around Flint until he found his favorite target a somewhat isolated liquor store. He went in and ordered a bottle of bourbon. When the clerk approached the counter at the point of a pistol, Josh ordered him to stop, and to keep both hands up above his waist.

He then asked him to remove all the currency and place the bills with the whiskey in a bag. The clerk complied. Josh told him, "That's fine. You did it right; and now if you will walk me to the door and sit down on that bench over there until I am out of sight and stay there I will not kill you as I have done many times in the past. They wouldn't stay down on the seat. It's not your money so you have nothing to lose except your life. Just stay seated about three minutes and I will let you live."

Josh walked out with the clerk and then after the clerk was seated and told to look the other way for three minutes he quickly ran to the side of the store where his car was parked with the motor running and the clerk remained on the bench looking the other way until the car disappeared down the side street. A new customer approached the store and witnessed the car speeding away. When the police arrived after the clerk called them, the clerk described Josh as a homeless looking guy with long hair and told them that the robber had told him to stay seated and to look the other way else be killed. He also told the police that the robber had told him that he had killed many people before who didn't cooperate. He told the police that the owner of the store advised his clerks to always obey the robber and as he was instructed he had placed a $20.00 bill on the top of a pile of $1.00 notes and also kept a separate stack of ones, fives, and a few tens to make the haul look like more money. The other high value notes were always deposited in a slot under the counter that dropped into a locked metal box at the time of the sale. He stated that the camera should have the entire event on film.

Josh returned to his room and emptied the bag on the bed. He counted a total of $173.00. "I'll be damned; I should have shot that cheap skate." He had seen the camera and realized that his appearance had to be changed once again.

They are surely looking for him now as a long haired whiskered individual. He got out of bed and cut and shaved his beard off. In the morning he went to a barber shop and had his hair trimmed crew style. He did not look like the same man. He went into a sporting goods store, and bought himself a baseball cap with the Detroit Tigers emblem on its front and a jacket with the Detroit Piston's logos on it.

His identity was changed once again. But he was still in need of cash. He had to get a lot more cash now that he had to stop using his credit card. He drove all about town until he found what appeared to be an easy place to get a large amount of cash. He knew that after this caper he would need to be on the run for possibly some time. He found a small grocery store and its parking lot was full of cars. It was a rather small store, but it was very busy. There must be a lot of cash in there he thought. It was probably the only store in the small town.

He went to a restaurant in the same mall where he could watch the parking lot and had dinner passing the time to wait for the store to prepare to close. He had already visited the store to get a feel for its layout. He failed to see any video cameras. There were three registers and a floor safe that was off to the side of the front windows near what appeared to be an office. It was locked of course.

The closing time was posted as 9:00pm. At 8:45pm Josh went back in the store and walked to the back of the store and started fingering through the cheese selections. The store lights eventually started to dim and Josh walked to the front of the store with a package of cheese. He went into the quick lane designed for less than 10 items. The three cashiers were closing down their registers and what appeared to be the store manager or head cashier, was taking the cash trays from each clerk and placing them on a cart evidently for storage in the safe which was still locked. Josh had purposely delayed his check out by purposely dropping his wallet on the floor and bending over to pick it up again.

The cart was now waiting for the drawer from the express lane and the cash cart was very near the last register, Josh reached in his jacket pulled out his gun and ordered the cashier to place all the folding money in all of the trays into a grocery bag at the end of the counter, and ordered him to open the safe. The cashier did as he was told and placed all the money in the safe in the same bag. Josh was pleased – this was a sizeable haul. Using his silencer fitted gun he shot the cashier and the remaining clerks, a total of four employees. Only the head cashier was shot with a fatal shot, the other three were shot in the lower abdomen, but they could not move.

Josh left the store with his two grocery bags, and took off in his conveniently parked auto. There was no one in sight as he pulled out of the grocery parking lot.

He drove on back streets at a slow speed, turning several times to make sure he was not being followed, and then went to his motel.

His evening was very profitable. The proceeds would carry him for several months. He was watching the late evening news and heard the report. The manager of the grocery was declared dead at the scene and three employees were in the hospital and all were reported in stable condition. The suspect had not been apprehended and there were no witnesses, except the three cashiers who were all in the hospital.

The suspect was reported to have been clean shaven. With a baseball cap that was pulled low on his forehead. The suspect was Caucasian about 6 feet tall and approximately 30 years of age. An artist's picture was displayed and Josh was happy that it was a poor likeness of him and there was no mention or indication of the scar on his cheek. It was also added that the suspect may have been a Hispanic as he was dark skinned. "Oh great that's a help in my favor." Josh thought.

The police made a note of the confession that Josh had given to the liquor store clerk, and set out a note to all area police stations and asked them to contact the Flint Police, if they had unsolved robberies or murders, especially those of liquor store employees. When the flyer came in on this new grocery store robbery, the FBI team in Midland decided to show its' pictures of Josh to the three grocery store clerks in Flint to determine if Josh could be the one who robbed the grocery and killed it's manager. None of them thought that their thief was found in the pictures show.Flint received a total of five such reports on liquor store robberies. When the description of that robber was received in Midland, the long haired homeless type, Bob forwarded them pictures of the artist enhanced drawings of Josh, and asked them to show the photos to the witnesses or victims for comparison.

One report came back, that stated that their suspect was seen leaving the scene of their murdered person and he did have shoulder length hair. They had no other information. The other report that came back was from the Flint robbery and that store clerk stated that the photo was the same as the picture with the short hair, even though he had a hat on. He added that his robber had a scar on his cheek. This was the clerk that was on the express window.

Bob went to Flint to get a positive ID from the liquor store employee that was told to sit and to turn away from Josh as he left the store. Perhaps he could positively identify Josh or identify his vehicle used etc. Bob was told that the car was definitely maroon in color, but the clerk did not know any part of a tag number, the state licensed, or the make of the car. He was too scared to turn his head too far.

The picture of Josh was also shown to the three grocery store clerks in the hospital and one of them identified a picture of Josh as the one who shot her. Bob was now certain that Josh had cut his hair and shaved off his whiskers.

He called Mary and told her, "Mary we are close on the trail of Josh. Please pack a bag for a week and get ready to leave for Boise and stay at my mother's house. I called Chief Herles and he told me that he would take you and the children to the airport. We are sure that Josh is in the area."

"But Bob, the children are in school. Have you talked with your parents?'

"Yes all the arrangements have been made. Sweetheart, I hate to ask you to do this again, but I just want to make sure that Josh will be unable to get to you or the children." "I understand Bob, but what about you, why don't you let the team handle the situation and you come with us?"

"Mary, you know that I can't do that, it's my job to protect you and the children, and my job to get this situation closed. We are getting close and I want to see that son-of-a-bitch in jail." "I understand Bob, I sure will be glad when all of this is over. Do you know it has been almost four years with us in constant fear of our lives and the lives of our children? Why don't we make plans on going to up to Rose Lake for a weekend when all of this is over, like we did prior to our getting married?"

"That's a date Mary."

"Wouldn't it be fun to go skinny dipping again?

That was fun wasn't it? I have to go now Mary, I will call you tomorrow when I get back to Midland."

"OK, dear, but please be careful."

"Goodnight. Tell the kids, I love them and I will see them tomorrow before you all leave."

"I will. I love you too. Goodnight."

Josh left Flint for a return to Midland. He was determined that he would put an end to the chase this time. He stopped for the night in a town about 25 miles west of Midland and checked into a motel. He picked up a Midland newspaper and an article on the first page caught his attention. "LOCAL MAN BACK FROM THE DEAD! Josh Merrill thought to have been killed in a fiery automobile 5 years ago, is wanted for murder and was a suspect in the killing of three persons, one in Michigan and one in Pennsylvania and another in Delaware. He was also a suspect in a fatal robbery of a grocery store in Flint. The story went on to mention his alias as Joseph Miller, his military service, and the repeated charges of harassment of his former wife, Mary Mitchell."

Josh was shaken. His plan on returning to Pennsylvania and to marry Ellen was probably impossible now that his ID as Joe Miller was exposed. He was going to call Ellen tonight but that too was out of the question. Her phone most certainly would still be bugged as it was when he lied to her about going to Canada. He knew the police heard that message.

He hoped that they had done so, because if they

thought that he was in Canada, his plan to settle his score with Bob and Mary would perhaps lessen their surveillance in Midland. If his plan was handled properly he would try to find a way for him to get with Ellen again.

Did she think that he had killed Wayne? If he and Ellen could get together he could hopefully put an end to his obsession. Now that he was also a suspect in the Flint grocery robbery and murder he decided that he must lay low for a time until things cooled off. He drove all the next day and headed for Kentucky where he checked into a motel and played the part of a salesman but spent most of his time in several bars.

After two weeks he decided that he had to put an end to this life on the run and decided that he would return to Michigan and put an end to the matter. He drove back to Michigan and observed that the lights were on at Bob and Mary's house and things looked as if all was OK to make his move. There appeared to be no surveillance.

I have to make my move quickly and then I can start all over again with another new ID. He thought to himself. His new plan had to be put into action quickly. He went to an Office Depot store and bought the largest cardboard box they had on the shelf, a roll of tape, and a package of mailing labels. He then returned to his motel room and assembled the box to appear as an addressed box .The label read Mr. and Mrs. Robert Mitchell. He would be In Midland by mid afternoon.

His plan now was to take a cab to a van rental firm. Pick up the large box at his motel to deliver it to the Mitchell residence. The box would have nothing inside and would be light in weight but its size could be used to hide his face. He planned it to appear that he was making a delivery.

He rented a panel truck and left his car at his motel and picked up the box and loaded it in the van. He drove to Mary's former house. He was unaware that she and Bob had moved into a new home some distance away and saw a new name on the mailbox at the street and then decided to check the telephone to see if he could get their new address. He found a pay phone and looked up their name. Sure enough it had their new address.

He drove past the new address several times in opposite directions and could see no sign of any surveillance being made. There were no cars parked anywhere on the street, and there were no cars parked in any driveways. The coast was clear.

The mail box at the curb simply had the house number on it and the words "The Mitchells." He took the package and walked up to the door. There was no answer and he had expected none as he knew they were both at work. He walked around to the back of the house carrying the parcel and found a screen enclosed porch. He neatly cut the screen wire on the door and went into the porch and broke a glass panel out of the rear door and entered the house. His plan now was to wait for Bob or Mary to come home. He went upstairs and found a window in one of the bedrooms with a clear view of the front yard and street where he could watch all the activity. His van was still there but no one was giving it any attention. He had purposely parked it across the street between two houses at the curb.

It was now just two o'clock in the afternoon, so he sat back and waited. He expected that the wait would be at least two hours before Bob or Mary would come home. He went down to the kitchen found a beer in the refrigerator and took the beer back to the bedroom window to wait for his targets.

At 2:30 he saw a car stop in front of the house and a little girl got out of the car and she came to the house. It was his daughter Nancy. My how she has grown he thought. His love for his girl almost let him rush downstairs to grab her in his arms, but he restrained himself until he saw the car leave after Nancy had opened and closed the front door.

He then quickly came up with a new plan. Nancy was his, and he would take her with him. He thought that he could put all of this mess behind him. He had lost Mary, and Billy was not his anyway. Surely he could close the case now. He would take what was justly his and disappear.

He went down stairs and found Nancy in the kitchen. After four years she still recognized him by pictures and yelled, "Daddy is that you, they told me you were dead?"

"Yes Nancy it is me. I was lost for awhile but I am home now. Let's go pick up your mother at the library and we can all go get some ice cream and sit down and talk about where I have been. OK?"

"Yes, daddy Billy and mom will both be happy to see you again. I can't wait."

They went out to the van, and drove on to the motel, where they got out of the van and got into his car. They drove out of Michigan. Josh knew that Amber alert would have the message up on the main highways in short order. He left the main roads and worked his way out of state and into northern Ohio and stopped at a motel in Findley, Ohio. He apologized to Nancy about the ice cream telling her that he had forgotten that he was to go somewhere to get a present and that they would all get together later.

Nancy was concerned that they had not picked up her mother and Billy as Josh had told her he was going to do, but he kept her talking and promising her a good time and they would all be together in a few days. She was so happy to see her dad she thought of nothing else.

Back in Midland, Mary arrived home and found that Nancy was not there, and discovered a huge empty box on the back porch and a broken rear window. She put in a panic call for Bob at the station.

"Bob, he has her —- Josh has my little girl Nancy, please come home."

"Mary, are you sure he has Nancy. How do you

know it was Josh?" Without waiting for a response he said, "I'll be right home."

Bob went home immediately and took three members of the FBI team with him. Immediately the team and Bob were questioning her. Mary told them that Janice had dropped Nancy off after school as she had been doing for over a month, and that she had waited for Nancy to enter the house before she left. She dropped her office at 2:30 so she disappeared between then and 4:15 when Mary arrived home.

Mary was upset because she always called Nancy at 3:00 to 3:15, and today she had missed the call because she was in a library staff meeting.

The FBI team leader asked two of his men to immediately contact the neighbors to determine if they had witnessed any activity around the house that afternoon. One of them came back in and said that she had seen a black van parked across the street, that it was now gone, but she had not seen when it left or who was in it.

Another agent reported that the lady who lived in the house immediately in back of Mary and Bob's home heard some glass being broken but when she looked out her window all she saw was a man who was delivering some packages and she assumed that he had dropped something.

On hearing that, the team leader called the station and told his team to initiate a kidnapping alert immediately. Bob talked with the police staff and an alert was issued to look for a black van. Knowing Josh's past record in renting vehicles when he was active he asked them to check with all rental firms in the area and to check the motel and hotel parking lots.

Within an hour the van was located at a motel and it had been abandoned there. Bob and the team assumed that he had switched cars there and was now in another vehicle. The media was alerted of the kidnapping and pictures of Josh were published in the newspaper and appeared on TV that evening as the suspect. Nearby police from all surrounding states were alerted of the incident and they were asked for their assistance.

The doctor arrived and gave Mary an injection to ease her anxiety.

Chapter Seven

Josh and Nancy stopped at a McDonalds Fast Food restaurant and ordered at the To Go Window their evening meal. Nancy asked if she could have milk and a slice of pie in addition to the hamburger and fries. He told Nancy that they would go back to the motel and write her mother a nice long letter to explain why they could not stop and see her yesterday as he had promised Nancy. He had not figured out yet what he could say that Nancy would understand without becoming upset.

They ate their meals and Nancy hopped into her bed and was asleep in a few minutes. Josh, then found some stationary in the nightstand and an envelope. The stationary was imprinted with the motels address which Josh cut off before he started to write his letter. The return address on the envelope was marked through with ink to the point that it could not be read.

Josh wrote and addressed the letter to Mary.

"Mary Louise there has been a change in my plans. I now have with me everything that is truly mine. I realize that I have lost you. Billy of course is not mine as you well know, and his father has already paid for his sin. While I hate Bob with a passion, I have come to realize that killing him would really serve no purpose to me and I suppose that he will provide well for you. I have met another lady myself, and she will make a great mother for Nancy."

"So all I ask for, in this ransom letter, if anyone wants to call it such is absolutely nothing. I have with me the only thing left in this world that means anything to me. and I will not share her with anyone. I dearly love her. I am now dropping out of your life and will start living again. You will never hear from me again, no threats, no offers to come back with me. I want nothing at all but peace and out of your life."

"I just ask that I be allowed to disappear. I will get a new ID, go to work, marry my new lady friend and we will bring my daughter up well. I will see that she is well educated, treated as she should be treated, a real lady. I promise you no harm will ever come to her. You once told me that I was a big shit. I will never be looked as such again. I have learned from my past. Money is no longer a problem. I have learned how to make money easily and I will invest it wisely. You will no longer need to put money away for Nancy, she will attend a university of her choice and I promise you that. Goodbye Josh."

"PS: Nancy is asleep at this time. Josh will disappear when this letter is mailed and reaches its destination. You can call off your surveillance. I am free at last."

In the morning Josh told Nancy that he was going to take her to a store and buy her some new clothes so that she would look pretty when Bob, Billy and her mother saw her next week. Her mother had been allowed to get off work in two weeks and after that they would all get together again.

He asked Nancy if she remembered boating and the winter vacations in Florida, Nancy said she did remember the boat. She drove it once. "Will we have time to go to Disney World or Epcot? "Could we all go boating again? I just wish Mommy didn't have to work at the library next week. I don't know why they wouldn't let her take off just one week."

The letter was dropped in a small post office's collection box in Kentucky.

When the letter was delivered to Bob and Mary, there was a visible sign of relieve when Bob read from the letter that Josh had promised no harm would come to Nancy.

Mary asked, "I wonder if she recognized Josh as being her father. Is she going with him willingly, you know we have never discussed Josh's problem with the children. If she does remember him, she has no knowledge of his obsession to kill all of us."

"Yes, that is true, but that may make things go easier with her capture, if Josh doesn't scare her and acts like a father. You told me once that Nancy did love him and perhaps that will keep her safe. I really believe that Josh will see that no harm will come to her in any way. I bet he thinks this matter is all over. We must make sure that he doesn't get out of our sights again. The FBI has experts on kidnapping and I am sure that they will find Josh soon, and we will have Nancy back with us unharmed soon."

"I do hope so Bob, but it seems to me that she will be wondering why we are not with Josh and her and that may irritate Josh. It might cause him to take his frustration out on Nancy. He has a very bad temper."

At the station, the FBI team was now headed by a so called kidnapping expert, an agent named William Stanton. His record of successful captures was outstanding. He reported that kidnapping of children by their divorced or separated parents rarely resulted in harm to the children other than the usual trauma.

That gave both Bob and Mary some relief. But he did go on to say that with Josh's apparent criminal activities, they had to be very careful because he was indeed a dangerous man.

He told the team the one thing that they did have going for them was that Nancy was now old enough to know right from wrong and that she would soon confront Josh where her mother, Bob, and Billy were and perhaps she would make an effort to contact them.

He instructed his team to instruct both Bob and Mary how to handle a contact, should Nancy attempt to do so. "Do you think she knows by memory your telephone number? Does she know your full street address?"

Mary replied, "I know she knows the library telephone number and I think she knows our home number. She called me at the library all the time. I think she knows our street address but I have no way of knowing that she does for sure."

Bob told the FBI, "She has called for me at the police station several times. She probably doesn't know the station number but in the past she always asked the operator to give her the police station. One time she did that on 911, and I told her never to do that again unless it was a real emergency."

Agent Stanton said, "Well I hope that she will try making a call when the suspect is not around. One problem with her calling is that she probably doesn't know the area code. If she were to call that would really give us a jump on him. It appears that he is heading East or South. This letter was mailed in Kentucky. I only wish we had a description of his car. "Couldn't we get a description from that girl whose husband was murdered that knew him as to make, color, etc of his vehicle?"

"I'll get on that right away Bill, but she said that he was in Michigan when her husband was murdered so we have no firm evidence at this point, other than their knowing each other that he had anything to do with her husband's death."

"Oh yes, I had forgot about that, Do not contact her

right now, but perhaps we can get the same information from where he worked. Let's try that first. Remember that he is a suspect in that murder and that he was a friend of the murdered man's wife."

"She said that she and her husband were just friends of Josh and that Josh, known to her as Joe, worked in the same garage as her husband. They just might know about his car."

Agent Calio said he would have the police in Elizabethtown, PA check on that right away and surely they could get that data from the garage owner or other employees. I am sure we can get the year and model of his vehicle from the Pennsylvania Department of Motor Vehicles. He probably had the car registered in the name he is using. I bet that his friends and the employer have that name for us. I bet I will have the name in a few hours."

In about 25 minutes they had their answer. Joseph B Miller was driving a red 1994 four door Nissan automobile and that it had Pennsylvania tags. There was a sticker on the rear bumper that advertising some message about the Florida Gators but exactly what the sticker said is not certain.

Agent Stanton said, "Hey that may be a clue as to where he is going. if he" roots" for the Gators he probably has some ties to Florida. Maybe he is on his way to Florida. I hope he is the one who put that sticker on his bumper.

Alert the offices in Florida, especially Orlando

and Tampa, he may be taking the girl to Disney or Busch Gardens to keep himself in good favor with the girl. Remember that Walker kidnapping case last year, Disney World was exactly where he took his daughter that he had kidnapped from his ex wife."

Josh and Nancy were in Tennessee when Nancy started asking her dad just when and where her mother, the baby, and Billy would be meeting them. "Can't you call them on the phone? I want to talk to her. Josh told her "Yes, we will call her this evening when we get to the place where we will be spending the night. OK? What baby are you asking about, did your mother have a baby?"

"Yes, we have a baby boy named Bobby. Pauline takes care of him during the day when mom works. But, I want to know why she didn't meet us as she promised you she would. I want to see them." "I told you honey. She had to stay at work and she could not get her vacation right away." "But why didn't we get to see her before we left for Florida. "I don't know, but we will ask her tonight." Josh was hoping that the conversation was over and that by night she would have forgotten about them. At dusk, they stopped at a restaurant for dinner and later found a motel just off the Interstate.

After checking in Josh turned the TV on and found a children's cartoon channel for Nancy to watch. He told her that he was going to take a shower and that she had better take one also after he finished his

He went into the dressing room and undressed and

got into the shower. Nancy saw a telephone on the night table and dialed her home telephone. The motel desk clerk told her that she would have to dial a 9 and a 1 and the area code before the telephone number. Nancy dialed but the call did not go through because she did not give the area code. She asked the Motel desk clerk to help her and told her it was a Midland Michigan number and repeated her home phone number.

The operator found the area code and placed the call for Nancy and the phone rang about three times when Bob answered the phone.

"Hello Bob, is that you, this is Nancy when are you all coming to Florida?"

Bob knew that it was Nancy and he was aware that the FBI was already tracing the call and that they were listening to every word. "Hello Nancy, are you OK, where are you honey?"

"I'm not sure where we are now we are on our way to Florida. Dad is going to take me to Disney World and I want you all to go to.""Honey, where is your dad right now?

"He's taking a shower." The FBI team gave Bob the sign that they had the trace.

Mary was now near the phone and demanded to talk to Nancy, but the FBI agent told her to listen only this is all being taped and we will soon know just where she is."Nancy honey, your mother is not here right now, but we will see you soon. I have to go to work now. Goodbye sweetheart. we will call you back in about an hour." Bob stopped the conversation and hung up. Mary was frustrated that they had not allowed her to talk to Nancy.

Agent Stanton explained to Mary that Josh was taking a shower and was probably unaware that Nancy was calling them and they wanted her off the phone before he got out of the shower. The call had originated at a Holiday Inn in Murfreesboro, TN and it would only be a very short time before agents would be on the scene. Nancy hung up the phone and was upset that she had lost contact but decided that Josh had told her that they would call back so she would just wait to talk to them again later.

When Josh was back in the bedroom area he told Nancy to take her shower. He then changed the noisy comedy show off and switched to the news channel.

Nancy said "OK, I didn't get to talk to mommy, we got cut off. "

"What do you mean? Did you call your mother on the telephone?"

"Not exactly, I tried to but Bob answered the phone and we didn't get to talk because we got cut off. I wanted to know when she will meet us in Florida."

"Oh dear Nancy, you should not do that again. How did you get the telephone number?" "I knew the number but I was having trouble getting it to ring, so the operator lady on the phone helped me. She did it for me."

"Did you get to say anything to Bob?"

"Yes, but he had to go out he's a policeman and has to go out quick all the time. I only told him we were on our way to Florida."

Josh was beginning to panic. He was certain that the telephone call had been taped by the FBI. They always do that when there is a kidnapping. They do it all the time like in the movies. He thought. I have to leave here at once.

He told Nancy. "You can shower later. I just thought of something. We have to leave here right away. To meet them on time, we have to leave and drive for a few hours, so we won't be late when they get there." Nancy was upset and asked "When are we going to meet mommy?" "Very soon honey unless we are late. We better hurry. Are you ready to go now? You better use the bathroom before we leave. I'll pack our bags OK."

"OK dad, but how will Bob know how to call us like he said he would?"

"He knows where we will be."

They loaded their bags and Josh decided to head North instead of South and planned to drive to Pennsylvania the next day. He stopped near Nashville and they spent the balance of the night in another motel. He wrote a letter to Ellen in Elizabethtown, telling her that he wanted her to meet him in Camp Hill, PA at the Farm Market's Dairy Barn on Highway 15 on Thursday at 12 noon. He added that he had been awarded custody of his daughter and he wanted Ellen to join them on a vacation trip.

He told Ellen that he was afraid to stop at her house, if the police wanted to talk to him, as she had told him earlier. I am AWOL from the air force and I don't want them to find me. He said he only had a week of vacation time left and he didn't want to be tied up with them until after his vacation time was over. So please don't tell them about this plan. I want and need you to help me with my daughter Nancy. I love you.

Please be at the Dairy Barn at noon where they sell ice cream and I will find you there. Remember don't tell anyone, I don't want to be interviewed about my military AWOL problem at this time. I can do that after we get back from Florida. I want to take Nancy to Disney World before I go back to the airbase.

When the FBI got to the motel in Murfreesboro, Josh was gone. It had been only 24 minutes since they traced the call. Josh had most likely found out that Nancy had made the call. Mary was taken to the hospital and sedated.

Ellen received her letter on Tuesday morning. She made notes of what Josh had written and was concerned about meeting Josh under such strange conditions. Was there something that Josh had not told her? Could he have killed Wayne? No, she knew he was out of state and she had talked to him on the phone from there the very evening that Wayne had been murdered.

He had mentioned a problem with the military and the police had told her that they wanted to talk to him about something with the military. She called the policeman that was working with her on Wayne's murder and told him that she was wondering just what that problem was. Did it have anything to do with Wayne's murder?

The officer came to her house and explained to her that Joseph B Miller was AWOL. He had simply left the base where he was stationed and never returned. He had no record of criminal activity while in the military, but he was a suspect in a harassment case, and that he was a suspect in a murder charge in Delaware.

Ellen, said, "Oh no, I don't believe that."

The officer did not mention that he was also a suspect in the murder of her husband. He went on to say, "Why are you concerned about his problem with the military?"

"Well, I just got to thinking about what you all said about wanting to talk to him about his military record. I was concerned that he may have had something to do with Wayne's death. They were very close friends and I know of no reason why he would kill Wayne. Could Wayne have been involved someway with Joe's problem and that may have been why he was murdered?"

"No, Ellen, we don't think that Wayne was involved with Joe's problem, but he may have found out that Joe was AWOL. We did check on him and we found out that he was out of the area when Wayne was killed. He left two days before the murder as I recall. Joe's landlord said that he had left two days before Wayne was murdered, but they had no evidence other than the landlord's statement to confirm that. He had not used his credit card since he left Elizabethtown. The police did not tell Ellen there was no proof that he had left early or that they decided to put a surveillance team on Ellen's residence.

"I think that you should come down to the station so we can tell you the complete story. Joe is a very dangerous man. You should be very careful if he ever contacts you again and if he does contact you again, you should let us know right away."

"I just got a letter from him today. That is why I called you. I was concerned."

Ellen was relieved when the police told her that he was on his way to Michigan when Wayne was murdered. She did love Joe, or whatever his real name was but if he was a murderer she wanted no part of him. A team of FBI agents contacted her within an hour and when they asked her to go ahead and arrange the meeting as Joe had asked. They had promised her full protection as they would be there when he made contact with her. She had nothing to fear. She was also told that if she did not cooperate, she could possibly be charged with aiding a criminal.

She decided that she would meet him at the Farmer's Market Dairy Barn south of Camp Hill, PA as he had asked her to do. She would hire a taxi to take her down there so she wouldn't have a problem with the car when she met Joe. She wondered how old his daughter was. Joe had never told her.

The FBI were alerted by the Elizabethtown Police Chief after Ellen had contacted them asking for information on Joe Miller.

Because of the fact that her husband's murderer was still on the loose with no leads, they had put surveillance on her around the clock because Joe was a suspect in that murder. A plan for his capture was formulated after Ellen had agreed to cooperate with them.

Josh and Nancy arrived in Camp Hill on Wednesday night and went across the river to Elizabethtown and drove past his apartment building and Ellen's house. There was no visible evidence of any surveillance at either place but he decided that he would not chance a stop at either location. He was unaware that the house across the street from Ellen's which was for rent, earlier in the week, was now occupied. The FBI was watching Ellen's every move.

He went back across the Susquehanna River to Camp Hill and found a little restaurant in the mall, where they had dinner. After dinner they went to the mall and he bought Nancy a few dresses and a back pack to put some of her books and doll items in that she had been accumulating during their travels over the past week.

Back at the motel, Nancy again began talking about wanting to see her mother.

Josh called her to come over and sit beside himself and told her that he had some bad news for her. "Nancy honey, I suppose that you are wondering why we changed our plans about going to Florida to meet your mother."

"Yes, I am daddy. I'm tired of riding, I want to go home and see mommy." Well darling, that is something we cannot do now. If I used the word divorce, would you know what I was talking about?" "Yes, daddy that is when two married people quit living together. Grace's parents are divorced and she lives with her mommy and her brother Tommy lives in Texas with his daddy. They don't live together now, but see each other some time. Are you and mommy divorced daddy, is that what you are telling me?"

"Yes, honey that is exactly what I am telling you. You know your mommy thought that I had died in an auto crash and I was not killed but I was lost for a long time. Then your mother married Bob. When I found my way home, there was no place for me. So your mother and I decided to divorce each other and she took Billy and the new baby and I took you just like your friend Grace's parents did. We will still get to see each other from time to time. Bob is her husband now and tomorrow I will take you to see your new mother. Her name is Ellen. You will love her and she will love you too."

"I don't want a new mommy I want to stay with my mommy. I want to go home." "I know you do Nancy and I promise you that all of this will work out soon. You will be able to visit your mother often. But we have to wait for things to be worked out. I love you Nancy and I know that Ellen will love you too."

"I love you too daddy."

"I know you do sweetie , now you go to sleep and tomorrow, if all goes well, we will go on to Florida like we started to do, and we will all go to Disney World and Epcot. Won't that be fun?"

"Oh yes, daddy I remember going there when I was little. I took a ride in a cup. That was fun."

In the morning they had a late breakfast and then drove to the Farmers Market and parked in view of the Dairy Barn. It was just a little after 11:00 so they decided to wait in the car and were watching the cows that were grazing near a fence. Nancy was asking a lot of questions about cows. Why are some cows black and white and some cows are all brown?"

Josh said "I don't know, maybe the brown cows have chocolate milk."

Nancy laughed and said "Daddy that's not right. Brown cows don't have brown milk."

Josh had been watching all the people entering the Dairy Barn who were buying ice cream and saw no one that looked suspicious, then he saw Ellen get out of a cab and she walked into the building. It was almost noon. In a few minutes she came out of the building eating an ice cream cone and went to a bench that was used by anyone to use while eating their cones or Sundaes.

Josh and Nancy walked toward the bench and Ellen saw them. Ellen ran to meet them coming from the bench and gave Josh a big hug and a kiss. She then grabbed Nancy and gave her a big hug, and told her, "So you are Nancy, I have heard a lot about you. You sure are a pretty little lady."

Josh grabbed Ellen and whispered "I have missed you. Will you marry me?"

Ellen said "You know I will. When can we get married?"

Josh said "As soon as we get to Florida and I get settled into a new job down there. I want you to come with me now."

"Not right now Joe, I will have to pack my clothes and sell my car and there's a ton of things to do first, and I have to tell the police where I am going. They said I should not leave without telling them. Remember?"

"Yes, I know that Ellen, but I have a problem with the Military, and I can't have them locate me just now. It would mean a few years in prison for being AWOL.

"Daddy, I want an ice cream cone, can I go get one?"

Ellen answered for Josh, "I'll go with you Nancy, its right over there. Do you want chocolate or vanilla?"

"I'll have a dip of each."

Ellen said, "OK let's go" and the two of them started for the barn.

Josh said, "I have to go to the men's room and I'll meet you in the dairy barn in a few minutes."

The four men who were walking slowly toward them split up. Two of them followed Ellen and Nancy into the dairy barn and the other two continued walking toward Josh. Josh glanced at the two following him and guessed correctly, they were looking at him. He quickened his pace toward the rest room and he saw them quicken their pace also. He went into the rest room and crouched up on the toilet bowl in a toilet stall. He pulled his gun from his jacket inside pocket, opened the stall door and saw the agents with their revolvers in their hands. He shot both agents in the back before they could turn around.

He ran out of the restroom toward the parking garage telling another man who was going to the restroom, "You better watch out, there's a man in there with a gun and I think he shot somebody." The man stopped and walked over to a bench and sat down while he was watching the activity at the restroom.

Josh reached his car and sped off, leaving Ellen and Nancy at the farm. He drove off on a side road and worked his way back to Interstate 81 where he headed north. He had not been followed.

He was mad at himself for letting his guard down back there. He was certain that he had now lost both Ellen and Nancy. He correctly blamed Ellen for setting him up. She probably was told that he was a suspect in Wayne's murder. Now what could he do? He knew that Nancy would be taken back to Mary. That was OK. He drove until he reached Wilkesboro, Pennsylvania where he spent the night. Bob and Mary were on a flight to Harrisburg to pick up Nancy.

Chapter Eight

Josh was destroyed, his plans on starting a new life and putting his life on the run to an end were all shattered. After he checked into the motel he went to a nearby bar and tried to drink his problems away. He failed to do that and staggered back to his motel room. He would decide in the morning just what steps he should take now.

Bob and Mary picked up Nancy in Harrisburg, and had dinner before catching the first of three flights back to Midland.

Nancy was asking questions about her dad "what had happened to him back at the farm where all the cows were.

Mary told her that her Dad was ill and had been ill for a long time.

Nancy said, "Is that why he was lost so long and couldn't find us?"

Mary said "Yes sweetheart."

"Will he find us again mommy? I don't want to live with him and Ellen. "

"You will live with Bob and I, Nancy, I promise you that."

"And with Billy and the baby too? Dad was going to take me to Disney World and Epcot. Can we all go there some time?"

"Yes we will all do that soon. Your new dad, Bob, has promised that we will all go to Lake Rose soon. Would you like to do that too?" "Oh yes, we can go out in a boat there and I will steer it." Josh woke up with a terrible hangover. He decided to stay put for another day. He went cross the street from the motel to have a cup of coffee and breakfast. On the way in he bought a newspaper out of a coin dispenser.

After he ordered his breakfast he was reading the highlighted front page of the Wilkesboro Morning News as was his usual routine, and his eyes caught a small article that read "Kidnapper eludes police after shooting two FBI Agents but the child was safely returned to her parents unhurt.. See story Page A6.

He immediately went to page 6 to get the full article. He was surprised to read that the two FBI agents were still alive and in the hospital in critical condition. In the article was a complete recap of the event including his name listed in the paper as Joseph Merrill who was using an alias of Joseph Miller.

It stated that he was the father of the girl he had

kidnapped. She was 11 years old and she had been kidnapped in Michigan earlier that week. It stated that he was the suspect in at least five murders and that he had once again avoided his capture. There were no witnesses to the shooting but one witness who had talked with the kidnapper just after the shooting identified the kidnapper as one on an FBI list of suspects.

He stated that the kidnapper had told him not to go in the men's room because someone had fired some shots in the men's room and that he was running away from the building to the parking lot. He stated that he sat on a nearby bench to see what was happening and afraid to enter the restroom. He saw the kidnapper leave the parking lot in a red automobile. He did not get the tag number or state because he had no reason to do so.

He was anxious to see what was happening in the men's room because he saw two men running toward the building and one of them went in the building, and the other man went around to the back of the building and then went in the building also. Their guns were drawn.

The article made no mention of Ellen, but it did say that Nancy was in a separate building at the time of the shooting and had been taken into a room for her protection by the FBI agents after which they went after the kidnapper. She was unhurt and later taken to Harrisburg to be united with her mother and stepfather.

The rest of the article was dedicated to the story of

Josh's accident, his reported death, and his use of a stolen ID. He had been harassing his former wife and her new husband for several years. Josh was shaken and scared. His picture was in the article, but was of a time that he had long hair and a beard. The make and year of his car had not been described other then it was reported as having been a red car. He was afraid to even leave the restaurant. He looked about the tables, and saw no one looking at him.

He could see his car across the street, no one was around it. He paid for his meal, crossed the street, got in the car and found an auto rental agency which he drove by and down the street he went around the corner and parked the car. He had decided not to chance that the FBI didn't know about his new alias and the make and tag number of his car.

He then walked back to the lot and picked up a white four door rental and drove it to a shopping mall about a mile away and found the area reserved for mall employees and delivery vehicles.

He then called for a taxi from a pay phone and had the cab driver take him back to his motel. He then walked to his car around the corner where he had parked it. After making certain that there was no one looking at it or in the area, he drove his red car and parked it in the area that he had found earlier.

He then went to his rented automobile that was parked not too far from where he was, and drove away on Interstate 476 toward Philadelphia.

He was happy that he abandoned that car in Wilkesboro. He wondered how long it would be before it was found at that mall. He was hoping for enough time to get to Philadelphia where he could catch a bus or flight to a distant location.

He was tired of this life of running. He would again find a new ID, and he swore to himself that he would never again, contact his old family. He would find a new life. He had been obsessed in attempting to get back with his family but now he was certain that would never be possible. He had been very foolish. He would just have to get them out of his mind.

He would find a place where he could start all over again. He would find a new wife and start a new family. He would change. No more robberies or killings.

He had never been to any of the cities on the west coast. It would be a safe place for him to become a law abiding citizen once again. He decided that he would go to Oregon. He bought a bus ticket to Portland. He would then find a town where he would become Mr. Good Citizen. The first leg to his new place of residence in Oregon was to Chicago. He left an hour later. His rental car was left parked across town in a theater parking lot.

When Bob and Mary arrived back in Midland, they were met with a swarm of news reporters, TV cameras and they asked Mary and Bob for statements and pictures. Their story made the national news service

195

and TV that evening. Josh was on the FBI's 10 most wanted criminals list.

Six months later, Mary opened her mail box and was shocked to see a letter addressed to Mr. and Mrs. Robert Mitchell and family, and it carried a return address of Mr. Josh Merrill but failed to have any street or city listed. It only gave his name. The letter had been mailed in Los Angeles, California. Once again Mary called Bob at work and told him, "Bob, Josh is at it again. I have a letter from him. I'm afraid to open it. Will he ever give up?"

Bob told her that he would be home right away.

The letter was opened by Bob he read it to Mary

Dear Bob and Mary.

I realize now that I have caused you a lot of stress over the past few years. I am indeed sorry for having done that. I also realize that I was mentally ill caused by not your doing but because of my own actions.

I am writing this note simply to ask your forgiveness. I promise that you will never hear from me again and I assure you that my obsession to get my old family back has subsided. I have given up all hope of doing that. I realize that will never happen. I now have a new ID and I have met another young lady who I plan to marry next month. She has accepted my proposal.

I have a good job I have money in the bank, not much, but enough for our needs. My intended is a Catholic, and I have joined her church. I have asked the lord for forgiveness, and I now ask for yours.

When I saw Nancy and after spending several days with her and then losing her once again, I realized that it was best that I get out of her life and yours. I was crazy with having lost you. It came to me that I was creating problems for her that if continued would possibly do her damage for her entire life. For the first time since losing you, I am happy once again. I am not running and I am satisfied that you are happy with Bob, and that he is giving you and my child everything that I selfishly deprived you of and could never have given you.

My only regret is not being able to watch little Nancy grow up and the terrible things I have done since I left you all. I only hope that the Lord will forgive me. Please do pray for me. Have no fear I am now out of your life. Josh.

Mary said, "Oh I do hope he means what he says. I will pray for him this evening."

Bob said, "I hope so too, but he does have to pay for his crimes and we will continue to search for him so that he can never again commit the things he has done to you, the children ,and especially the families that lost loved ones."

Josh arrived in Portland, Oregon after spending time in Los Angeles to obtain a new ID. He was clean shaven, with no mustache, and had a crew cut haircut. He appeared to look about 10 years younger than he actually was. He followed the same routine that he had used on three previous ID changes. He was now successfully documented as Nicholas T. Wright.

He had found a small apartment and had paid the security deposit and the first month's rent with his new credit card. He had opened a bank account with the last of his cash, and he immediately started looking for a job. In spite of the economy that everyone was complaining about, he found three firms that were advertising for experience mechanics.

He was employed with the second firm for which he applied. The first firm had just hired the one position that they had an opening for and they told him that they would hold his application should they have the need for an additional mechanic. They told him that the man they hired was also a military mechanic with the US Army.

Josh was happy that he had been too late on the first position because the second firm was a much larger firm and had 12 mechanics. It was a Chevrolet agency, and Josh was well familiar with Chevrolet parts. He was assigned to the truck garage and that was his preference. After three months he was given a permanent position with an increase in salary and benefits that included his health care. He loved his job and made friends rapidly with the other mechanics. He became very friendly with a fellow mechanic name Harry Titus.

Harry was single and 4 years younger than Josh. He was an active party guy and invited Josh to attend several area bars which offered music, dancing and meals. They went quite often for dinner and spent the rest of the evenings dancing and drinking.

They did all the area bars but Josh soon found out that Harry was a one drink guy and never got out of line. He too began to cut his drinking and found out that like Harry, he was having more fun and more dance partners than he had ever before.

He met and danced with a very pretty girl close to his age. Her name was Lydia. She was a nurse and worked for an orthopedic surgeon. She had divorced her husband of four years. She had one child, a daughter name Hilda who was nine years old. Her husband turned out to be an alcoholic and refused to try rehabilitation.

He had left home after losing his job and disappeared for over a year. On his return they had tried to put everything back in order, but he just could not stop drinking and was killed in an auto accident when he ran through a railroad barrier and was struck by a train. He was not drunk at the time of the accident. The railroad gate had failed to lift and the warnings lights did not flash. Four people were killed, her husband, and three persons in another car approaching in the other direction.

She had received a settlement check from the railroad without suing, but a lot of that money was used to pay her husband's debts and the mortgage that she had been struggling with over the years.

She had only recently started going out dancing after many months of her best friend's urging. She was a Catholic and very active in church affairs.

Josh told her that he was Catholic also, but had not

been to a mass in years. She asked him if he would go to her church if she went with him. He agreed and this was the start of a new friendship. He attended church every week, visited Lydia's home frequently and was soon endeared by Lydia's daughter Hilda. Lydia told Josh that she was pleased that Josh had taken to her because Hilda had not had a father's influence. Josh was feeling like a family man again. Hilda reminded him of his own Nancy and once when they were all together, Josh made the mistake and called her Nancy. Lydia caught that mistake and asked Josh where he got the name Nancy from. He simply said, "Nancy, did I call her Nancy, I didn't realize I had made that mistake. It just came out. I was married once and had a daughter named Nancy." "Nick you know you have told me nothing about yourself. What went wrong with your marriage? Do you have any other children? "

"Yes Lydia, I was married at one time and had one daughter, her name was Nancy. I suppose that is where the name Nancy came from. I was married for a little over a year. We were divorced after I came home early from work one day and caught her in bed with my best friend."

The divorce was not contested. I could probably have got the child but there was no way that I could care for an infant. My wife took the child and went back to Kentucky to live with her parents. I suppose that it was with her parents. I have never seen or heard from her since the day of our divorce and my so called best friend left town a month or so later. They may be together for all I know."

Three months later, Josh and Lydia were married. They honeymooned in Hawaii.

For the first time since he left his family, he felt that things were going right for him. When they returned to Portland, and went back to work, Josh was advised that he was being considered for the position of Service Manager and would become an annual rate employee rather than an hourly rate employee and a week later he assumed the position.

Josh decided to celebrate the promotion and discussed over dinner at The Red Lobster, the possibility of buying a new home. Lydia was happy about that and told Josh that she had over $20.000 in a CD that was expiring in the next month, the last of her railroad settlement payment, and she would use that as a down payment, adding that was what she had been saving it for and also for her daughter's education. Josh told her that they could start building that savings back up.

She also told Josh that they could sell her house to decrease the mortgage they would require to purchase the new home. Josh told her that perhaps they should reimburse the savings account for Hilda when the house was sold and put some money in a savings account for their use in the future if needed and apply the rest on the mortgage when the house was sold. They decided that they would not buy the new home until they sold Lydia's house. Lydia was pleased that Josh had suggested that they would reimburse Hilda's education fund and that perhaps they should just wait to buy the new house until they sold the one they had. She had not thought about not using Hilda education fund and was pleased he was looking out for their future. Josh was proud of himself he had made a sound and wise decision.

Lydia's house was sold in the second month after listing it. Josh told the realtor that they must have listed it too low. The realtor told them that they got the market price for the home and that it sold rather quickly because there was a need for low cost housing. It was the middle range of housing that was hard to move.

They bought their new home and a mortgage was approved by the bank after Lydia and Nick, Josh's new alias,, paid a large down payment. Josh had decided to leave Hilda's money in the CD, and to place a total of $20,000 in a savings account for their use if need for an emergency and to use the remainder of the proceeds to apply to the down payment. They now had a total of $40,000 in two CD savings and a new home. Josh felt as if he were rich.

Two weeks later Josh talked Lydia into getting a second car so she wouldn't have to drive him to work every day. He withdrew $10,000 from the savings account and financed the balance. Two weeks later he was a week late on his first mortgage because he needed money to get his auto tags and auto insurance. On payday he was again up to date on all of his bills. The following week Lydia told him that she was pregnant.

Chapter Nine

Bob and Mary had not received any threatening letters from Josh after Nancy was taken away from him in Pennsylvania. The FBI advised Bob that there had been absolutely no clues as to where he was. They had recovered Josh's car in Wilkesboro, Pennsylvania three weeks after he had avoided capture in Camp Hill. He had parked the car at a mall where cars were always parked twenty four hours a day mostly by employees.

They said it was only after a security guard noticed that the tags had expired over a month ago and he posted a notice on the employee bulletin board that was never acknowledged and a ticket was placed on the car. The ownership was established and the police confiscated the car and notified the FBI. Wilkesboro was North and East of Camp Hill and indicated that he had traveled north from Camp Hill.

The FBI had contacted the auto rental agencies

in Wilkesboro because that was the routine that Josh always used to elude his captors and they checked all rental records over a week's time after the Camp Hill murders. They discovered that one rental was abandoned in Philadelphia. And that auto was rented by Joseph B Miller. The trail on Josh ended in Philadelphia, and he had not rented another rental in Philadelphia or any nearby rental firms using his credit card or the name of Miller.

Bob and Mary finally arranged to take a vacation for a week after school was out for the summer months and the family went to Rose Lake, as they had promised to do a few months earlier.. On the way to the Camp Ground, Bob asked Mary if she would like to go sailing on the Lake again as they had done before they were married. Mary replied "Yes that would be wonderful and fun." And the children agreed. Bob asked, "How about if we go up to the lake's north shore like we did once and take a swim?"

Mary smiling said "That would be fun but not like we did then."

Billy asked, "Why not, what did you do then." Mary and Bob both smiled and Mary said, "Well your dad had a hard time finding the bottom so he could stand up." Nancy said, "If you were swimming, why did you want to stand up? Bob simply replied as Mary smiled, "I wanted to stop swimming and look at the beauty in the area."Nancy added "Please lets go there I want to see what's so pretty. What's so pretty there?"

Bob said that there was a bird sanctuary there and there were lots of pretty birds. Nancy asked "Oh goody, can we go see the birds?

Mary said that they would be sure to do that while they were on vacation. Surprisingly they were assigned the same room that they had used earlier. Bob had not noticed but Mary reminded him. The room had a door that opened into the adjoining room where the two children slept. The baby had been left with her grandmother back home in Midland.

Bob's mother had insisted that she be allowed to sit the child for the week they were away. She was at last a blood grandmother but she never showed any partiality toward it. She loved all three of them.

Lydia gave birth to a little girl and asked Josh what they should name it. Josh suggested that they name the child Nancy. "Nancy Catherine Wright, yes that sounds great, my mother's name is Catherine. She will be pleased that we named the child after her. Where did you get the name Nancy Nick, was that a relative?"

"It's just a pretty name. I have always loved the name Nancy. The daughter of my previous marriage was named Nancy and she is now out of my life now. Do you think that we could name her Nancy anyway?

"I see no problem with naming her Nancy. It will be interesting what nickname her friends will give her when she gets a little older.

"I bet it will be Nan, or Kate or Cathy." His memory had drifted back to his daughter, Nancy Merrill. He wondered what happened after she was taken from him. Had she been told about me he thought. When he got her in Midland she had not been told anything about his letters or threats except that he had been killed in an auto accident. He was assured that with all the FBI and Police around her after he escaped, He was certain had she had been told. She will never go with me again. Then he began think of Ellen. He had truly loved her, but she had set him up and he was close to have been captured. The more he thought of the past he could feel his hatred building up all over again. If Bob had not married Mary, he was sure that he could have fixed up things with Mary. Once again he was obsessed with the thought that he had to kill Bob. He just could not get that out of his mind.

Lydia noticed a change in his behavior and finally asked him what was bothering him. He told her that he just had a lot on his mind and that he needed to take a vacation. The job was now getting to him he told her. "When I used to get up tight, I always went fishing by myself and forgot all my problems."

"Then why don't you take a few days off and do some fishing. Mother is here helping me with the baby and it would be a good time to do it."

"Are you sure you will be OK Lydia, I just might take a whole week of my vacation and go up into Canada and do some fishing up there. They tell me there is great fishing around Vancouver."

"Yes, that would be great, you need a rest and mother will be here for another two or three weeks."

Josh had worked himself up into a frenzy once again he was determined or obsessed with his need to punish Bob for marrying Mary and eliminating his chance of getting his family back together again. He realized that was impossible now and that he had come to enjoy his life with Lydia but felt that he would never have any total peace in his life until he had settled this thing with Bob.

He asked his employer if he could take a week of his vacation because he had a family problem come up and he needed to take some time off to handle it. His employer told him that was no problem business was slack anyway. Josh went home and told Lydia and her mother that he had been given a week off and that he was going to go up into Canada and do some fishing. Josh headed east toward Michigan and was excited that he at last was about to put an end to his obsession. He had already made up his mind that he was not going to play cat and mouse this time. He would send no letter to warn them as he had always done in the past. He was going to shoot Bob at the first chance when he was certain that his escape from the area was clear.

He stopped for the night and went to a bar to have a few drinks and went back to his room to work out a plan to pull off his settlement of the thing that was driving him insane. He could not sleep. He got up and dressed and then drove about the small town to settle his nerves. He drove past a small liquor store and decided that he could use some cash and he could use it pay some of his bills back in Portland. They were easy prey and he had always been able to get the money with little or no resistance. He checked his gun, and silencer that was in his trunk hidden under the spare tire.

He was getting excited and he drove back around the liquor store and parked directly in front of the store. He waited for a time when there was no one in view on the street or in the store. In this store there were many bottles of various liquors on shelving where customers could pick up the bottles they wanted and take them up front to the register.

He made a selection and checked the street to see if anyone was on the street near the store. Seeing none he walked to the register with a bottle of bourbon whiskey, sat it on the counter and pulled his gun and told the clerk to empty the register in a bag and he would not shoot him. The clerk, a man in his late sixties or seventies, complied as he had been instructed should such an event ever arisen.

Josh thanked him and told him to walk to the back of the store and told him to sit down and stay there for three minutes. Josh quickly rushed to his car and drove back to his motel. He counted his take and he had easily made a total of $423.00.

The liquor store clerk called the police and the store owner as soon as he was sure that the robber was gone. He explained to the police exactly how the robbery was made step by step mentioning that the robber had selected a bottle of bourbon and had brought it to the counter but that he had left it on the counter and left only with the money in a paper bag. Then the police man asked him if the robber was wearing gloves and the clerk said no. "Is that the bottle asked the police. Yes, the clerk said and started to pick it up but the policeman told him not to touch it. "The bottle is evidence and will be taken to the station for finger prints."

At the police station, finger prints found on the bottle were lifted and sent for a possible verification to the FBI.

A few days later The Midland Police station and the branch FBI offices were sent a message that a robbery in Baker City, Oregon bore the prints for a suspect that was on the list of the10 most wanted criminals. The name on the matching prints were of Joseph B Miller who was AWOL from the Dover Air force Base in Delaware and with matching prints also for Nicholas Wright who had been issued an Oregon Drivers license in Portland Oregon. They were and the same individuals. The FBI in Portland was immediately notified and an investigation on Nicholas Wright was ordered. It was determined that he was on vacation and was reported to be heading up to Canada to fish around Vancouver. One agent stated well he's not headed for Canada that's for sure, he's heading east. The Midland Police Department and Bob were alerted and the notice expressed concern that just perhaps Josh was one again heading for Michigan.

Bob's home was once again placed on a routine watch. Bob did not tell Mary because there was no evidence that pointed where he was heading and that they had no threatening letters as was usually the case. An inquiry at the banks in Portland came up with a credit card number that had been issued to Josh and if he used the card for gas they could determine where he was or where he was heading. Tracking him was now top priority for the FBI. He had seriously wounded two of their agents back East in Pennsylvania.

His automobile description and tag number were disseminated across the United States and was soon appearing on the Interstate amber alert messages.

Josh slept thru the night and was up early in the morning and was checking his maps to setup a route through south Idaho where he could pick up the Interstate 84. After breakfast in a nearby restaurant he returned to the motel to check out and picked up a motel guest free newspaper from Boise, Idaho. During the check out the clerk told Josh, "We had some excitement here last night there was an armed robbery of the town liquor store and a shooting in one of the bar rooms.. These were the first crimes we have had here in Baker City in a long time."

Josh asked "Was any one shot or hurt?"

Josh was surprised to hear about a shooting in the bar room he was unaware of that. He smiled because he thought that would take some of the pressure off the search for him.

"No. but the guy shooting in the bar was not trying to shoot anybody he was just mad about something somebody said, and started shooting in the air. He did shoot at a mirror and told everybody to get on the floor. Then he just ran out of the bar and took off running. "

The clerk that was held up in the liquor store told the police the robber was very polite and well dressed and that he had never seen him before. The police don't think it was the same man that was in the incident at the bar. Everybody knows everybody here in Baker City. They were both probably from out of town."

Josh thought that he was wise to have spent the night in Baker City, because the police would certainly be running up and down Interstate 84 as that was the only quick exit from the town. He thought for once things had worked out in his favor.

He called home on his cell phone and told Lydia that he was in Vancouver and was going fishing after lunch. He then left on his way to Michigan and late in the afternoon he stopped for gas and paid cash. He didn't want Lydia to ever question how a gas bill had been paid in Idaho.

As Josh approached Boise Idaho, he saw an amber alert message on the overhead sign and it caught his eye. It was his tag number and his auto description. Josh panicked he could not figure out how they got that information. He looked in the rear view mirror to see if anyone was close enough to him to read his tag number. He saw none and kept his speed set to stay away from any approaching vehicle.

He saw the next exit and turned off the interstate. He had no idea where he was or in which direction he was headed. He found a parking space and parked in to a position so that his tag could not be read. He had to get that Oregon tag off the car. That state stood out like a sore thumb. He removed the tags completely and drove off without any tags and after reading the map decided to head to the next small town and look for a place where he could remove an Idaho tag from some parked car and place them on his car.

Driving around the few streets in the town, he saw what appeared to be an answer to his tag problem. He found an old house that appeared to be closed up as it had numerous items on the driveway leading to the house with several newspapers still in their delivery plastic bag.

It was approaching dark so he found a little restaurant and ordered a burger and some fries to kill the time while waiting for dark. Within an hour he had removed the tags and placed them on his car and followed his redrawn route until he arrived at the Craters of the Moon tourist area, where he parked his car in a motel lot where he was to spend the night. It was very late and he had to wake the clerk at the motel. He was, for the first time, since he allowed his death to be faked, really scared. He was aware that if they had his Oregon tag and auto identification, that his wife Lydia was probably now aware that he was a wanted criminal.

He was back to where he started years ago. He had again lost his family, had lost his safe haven in the military, had lost his second chance with Ellen and now he had lost his second wife, and another daughter named Nancy.

He had committed several murders and robberies and had less than $500 in his pocket. All because of his obsession to kill Bob. He knew that it would now be only a matter of time before he was captured and sent to prison or executed.

For several hours he could not sleep. He had finally given up. He knew this had been his last chance to live a happy life. He decided that he was going to end his running. He was going to kill Bob and disappear once again for ever. No more killings or robberies. In the morning he left for Pocatello and got back on his original route. He wondered if Bob was aware of his present problems.

Two days later he was in Midland Michigan and drove past Bob and Mary's home. He saw nothing that would indicate that the house was being watched. On the second trip past the house he saw Billy come out of the house and ride away on a bicycle. He drove past the house once more and then parked down the street on the other side and parked. He had a clear view of the house. At a few minutes after 4:00pm he saw Mary drive up in her driveway and go in the house and about an hour later he saw what he was waiting for. Bob drove up and parked his car along side of the car Mary was using, and when Bob got out of his car he went into the garage and moved a girls bicycle out of his way and then returned to his car to pull it into the garage.

Josh started his car and pulled up the street and stopped at Bob's driveway. He hollered "Hello Bob" and Bob turned toward him. Josh pointed his gun at Bob and shot.

Bob fell to the ground just as a police cruiser drove past Josh in the other direction as Josh was leaving the scene. He saw the shooting and rapidly turned his patrol car around, radioed for an ambulance to Josh's house immediately, and then announced that he was chasing the suspect. He gave his location and direction and asked for help.

Within a few minutes three patrol cars had joined the chase and were approaching the main highway away from Midland, heading north. The cars were all travelling in excess of 90 miles per hour and were approaching a sharp turn when Josh was about to pass a slow moving truck.

Josh lost control of his car when a car was approaching from the opposite direction. Josh missed hitting the approaching car but went off the road and over an embankment to the forest below where the car burst into flames.

Mary gave Bob the local newspaper the next morning in the hospital where he was recuperating following surgery on his upper chest to remove a bullet that had struck his police badge before penetrating his chest. The headline read Josh Merrill killed in a fiery crash within sight of where he was reported killed years ago.